CAPTAIN OF THE STEPPE

CAPTAIN
OF THE STEPPE

Oleg Pavlov

Translated by Ian Appleby

Introduced by Marcel Theroux

First published in the UK in 2013 by
And Other Stories
91 Tadros Court, High Wycombe, Bucks, HP13 7GF, United Kingdom

www.andotherstories.org

ISBN 9781908276186
eBook ISBN 9781908276193

A catalogue record for this book is available from the British Library.

Supported by the National Lottery through Arts Council England.

This publication was effected under the auspices of the Mikhail
Prokhorov Foundation TRANSCRIPT programme supporting translations
of Russian literature.

CONTENTS

Dedicated to Russian captains, those strongest of servicemen, on whose hard graft, aye, on whose hard graves our Empire-state reposed through the centuries. May they never be forgotten.

INTRODUCTION

The steppe where this story unfolds is the vast grassy plain which sweeps across the heartland of the former Soviet republic of Kazakhstan. In Kazakh, it is known as Saryarka, the yellow steppe. It is a place vividly recreated in Oleg Pavlov's novel – its endless grass, its changing light, its mud, its snow, and the fierce Buran wind that blows over it in winter.

The Kazakh steppe forms part of the vast Eurasian steppe which rolls between Russia and its former empire in Central Asia. It is a place of bewildering size. I have crossed parts of it by train and by air. Its hugeness is disorienting. In such a landscape, individual human beings and their struggles seem diminished in dignity and significance.

During Soviet times, the Kazakh steppe was a place of exile and punishment. Prisoners served out their sentences doing forced labour in the notorious Karlag system of camps, which centred on Karaganda — a city proverbial in Russian for being in the middle of nowhere.

In *Captain of the Steppe*, Pavlov's subject is the lives of the most transient and isolated of the steppe's inhabitants: a company of soldiers at a remote penal colony during the last decade of Soviet power. The men are guarding prisoners — in camp slang, *zeks* — at an outpost in Karabas, forty or so kilometres from Karaganda. The *zeks* are almost certainly mining coal for Soviet factories. In fact, the prisoners themselves are dealt with only glancingly. Pavlov's main interest is in the lives of a handful of the soldiers, in particular Captain Ivan Yakovlevich Khabarov, who is the book's hero.

A decent and conscientious officer, Khabarov is coming up to his retirement. A more pragmatic man would see out his final days at the camp and leave. Not so Khabarov.

The American novelist Kurt Vonnegut laid it down as a principle of good storytelling that 'every character should want something, even if it is only a glass of water'. The desire that moves Khabarov is just as primal and only slightly more grandiose. Frustrated by the rotten rations sent out to his troops along with year-old copies of *Pravda*, he is inspired to find a solution. The plan he comes up with is very simple: he decides to grow a crop of potatoes in order to feed his men.

Despite his ignorance of agriculture and the reluctance of the hungry troops, who can't see the sense in burying something you can eat, Khabarov perseveres with his scheme. And as he is repeatedly thwarted, his sensible and humane plan begins to take on the dimensions of a tragicomic obsession.

Khabarov's single-minded pursuit of his mission triggers a series of unexpected episodes, misunderstandings and unforeseen outcomes that could be called farcical if the novel's overall key wasn't so resolutely minor. Most significantly, he finds himself pitted against the shady special investigator Skripitsyn, a man whose opponents have an unfortunate tendency to perish in fires.

During his military service in the 1980s, Oleg Pavlov himself worked as a camp guard in northern Kazakhstan, and the book is packed with the kind of detail that assures us of the author's experience in this world. Pavlov confidently recreates the soldiers' slangy and abrasive speech; he is a connoisseur of the malodorous atmosphere of the camp, the operations of the latrines, and the bathhouse which smells 'as though they were drying out damp cats'. There is a note of personal bitterness when he compares a character to one of 'those medical orderlies, posted to obscure military hospitals . . . who, if they treat you, will surely cripple you'.

Captain of the Steppe was first published in Russia in 1994, when its author was twenty-four, and became the first in a loose trilogy about the lives of men working in the prison system of Soviet Kazakhstan. It is an almost purely male world. Female characters in *Captain of the Steppe* include only a telephone receptionist, a train driver, a faithless wife and some Kazakh women encountered during wanderings on the steppe. The book has a young man's relish for ribaldry and knockabout humour, but there is pathos too.

Pavlov does not aim for a naturalistic depiction of the life of the camp – the sort that is so hauntingly achieved in the stories of Varlam Shalamov. Instead, Pavlov imbues his world with a very particular flavour: the mixture of tragedy, absurdity and black comedy that runs in the veins of Russian literature as far back as the work of Nikolai Gogol.

The spine of the story is Khabarov's mock-heroic quest for his potatoes, but Pavlov has a Gogolian fondness for excursions into the lives of his minor characters: the morose Cossack Ilya Peregud, who knows how to make vodka out of 'rice, wheat, rotten apples, wood chips, old women's headscarves or sour cabbage soup'; the villainous Skripitsyn and his hapless sidekick Sanka Kolodin; or the incompetent Colonel Pobedov, who presides over an organisation which enacts in miniature the failings of the entire Soviet system:

> By then he already considered himself an eminent military commander, not knowing – because they weren't reporting it to him – that the soldiers were escaping from the companies and the *zeks* from the camps, where the guards standing sentry were drunk and asleep; that the officers were fighting over the most insignificant appointments and promotions, while in the more distant locations there

were unholy levels of drunkenness; that everywhere the very plaster was coming away.

Hanging over the book is the knowledge that, within a very few years, the Soviet Union will cease to exist, and the province in which the prison camp stands will become part of the newly independent nation of Kazakhstan.

Captain of the Steppe can be read as a satire on the absurdity and chaos of the decaying Soviet empire, but in the end it is Captain Khabarov's struggle that stays in the reader's mind. He is an obsessed but decent individual trying to do his best in a world which finds his altruism both unfathomable and threatening. And in telling the story of Khabarov's obsession and its impact on those around him, Pavlov fashions a disquieting and comic elegy for the foot soldiers of a vanished nation.

Marcel Theroux
London, 2013

CAPTAIN OF THE STEPPE

1

ONCE UPON A TIME

They used to deliver newspapers like potatoes to the company stationed out in the steppe: a month's worth at a time, or two, or even enough to see them through to spring, so as not to waste fuel and not to pamper the unit. They were last year's papers, sent from the chaotic regimental reading room where they took whatever was left in the binders of back issues. But even though the papers were tattered, when they reported something big that had taken place long ago, unknown to the soldiers, they found tears could be squeezed from their eyes. To find out so late and yet so suddenly about all the world's events drove the soldiers to squander what remained of their lives; lives that were in any case wasting away. Even amidst this dereliction of duty, you could hear them drearily going over and over what they had read, reluctant to forget. Word by word, the discussions among the servicemen grew more heated, each man developing his particular opinion and, if suddenly some bigger and more significant event came to light, yet without any clear political line, it would end in fisticuffs.

Captain Khabarov expected nothing from life. If he ever planted himself in a group of these textual analysts, he would furtively mix his long-standing personal anguish into the general unease arising – or so they maintained – from the international situation.

Ivan Yakovlevich Khabarov had wound up in government service neither through calculation nor through coercion; mind you, his own free will hadn't played much part either. So they had shaved his head and taken him as a soldier, as they did everyone. He served out his time. But when his term as a conscript was up, they persuaded him to stay on as a sergeant major. 'Stay put, Ivan, carry on serving. This is the right place for you. You're not one of them civvy bastards, are you?'

The military man in Khabarov could be detected in his mean, crude features. The sergeant major was a thickset, stocky man who resembled a great sack of potatoes. This made him unremarkable, comparable to maybe another million servicemen just like him. However, this million formed a mass of people within which each individual disappeared without trace. He was fated – here's the truth – to be suspended in it like some sort of clot. Anyway, he stayed in the service for the rations and the pay packet, which wouldn't buy much in the way of treats. No matter what happened, Khabarov would think, 'There's no way around it; just have to put up with it.'

And he also thought, no matter what happened, 'This isn't over yet.'

Now in dusty captain's epaulettes, Khabarov was serving out the rest of his natural life in one of the camp companies in the Karaganda region. He'd been shunted around the prison camps from Pechora to Zeravshan for longer than any hardened criminal, yet he hadn't been promoted any higher.

The place in the steppe where Captain Ivan Yakovlevich Khabarov was now serving was called Karabas. This is what the Kazakhs had dubbed it. In their language, the name meant something like 'The Black Head'. However, there were by now no Kazakhs to be seen anywhere near Karabas. They had settled on far-off collective farms, raising sheep. From time to time the steppe-dwellers would come into the settlement for a quick look at the camp, and in the hope of maybe getting their hands on a bit of ironmongery. And when they were asked how the place had come to inherit such a dour name, the Kazakhs looked round shiftily and confessed that they didn't know where their forefathers had got this notion of blackness or how they had contrived to see a head in the midst of this desolate expanse of steppe. The hills that surrounded the place like grey smoke did not look remotely like heads, while their stony ridges darkened in the dank weather to look more like tree stumps. Mind you, there was space and to spare. No plant life, nor agriculture, nor rivers troubled the good steppe earth. There was no crowding. It wasn't because of the space, though, that people had settled there. They were to build a prison camp; the site was chosen as if someone had spat there, purely out of malice, and there they had set about living.

Karabas was divided into two parts, of which the more unassuming was the sentry company quarters, while the other, all too visible – like some great barge on the steppe – was the camp itself. Both the company quarters and the camp had been built at the same time, but they had suffered many batterings over the years, while temporary structures had been put up and pulled down with equal abandon. In all its time, the settlement had never seen shops, public amenities, houses or churches. There were only cheerless barracks, exactly like kennels, right down to the idiot howl of the guard dogs that echoed around them. Boots had trodden out pathways stretching towards the barracks. The paths were so narrow, it was as though people had been walking along a rim, afraid to fall. These paths led away to dead ends, breaking off where the sealed zones and other strictures began. Access to Karabas was by a narrow-gauge railway that parted company from the main line far beyond the hills. Another route away from the camp led to a barely visible graveyard, where the sickbay buried unclaimed *zeks*. At this site, from time to time, freshly dug soil would appear. These were all the connections, as it were, all the ways in and out. If truth be told, in Karabas only the barrack lice circulated freely, two-timing the soldiers with the *zeks* at will, and vice-versa.

The lice paid each other visits, eating and drinking, and multiplying a hundredfold. Meanwhile the men suffered from itchiness and squashed the little monsters in the midst of their festivities, which created a bond between them stronger than a mother's love.

Not counting the livestock, Karabas was inhabited by soldiers, *zeks*, volunteer workmen and prison warders. The *zeks* and the soldiers lived here for years, seeing out their terms, which meant military service for some and imprisonment for others. A small factory had been built in the camp where they knocked together boots, always to the same pattern, boots that weighed a ton, for just such camps as this. The working days exhaled sour cabbage soup; long and oppressive, they welled up as though from ancient depths.

The soldiers stayed alive on their pay and rations. There hadn't been a pay rise in decades, but there hadn't been a pay cut either. On the quiet, it's true, there were mutterings that they were long overdue a raise for this sort of service. On the basis that a substantial portion of their wages was being embezzled, they would serve still more slackly, so as not to lose out. Meanwhile their commanders were glad to take every opportunity to declare that they were carrying out their duties poorly and being paid for nothing. And that's where things were left. In the summer, rations would be cut to try and save at least a little something for the winter, while in the autumn, similarly, they wouldn't get quite enough, as rations were kept aside, in reserve. But when January stole up unannounced, these reserves would barely feed a sparrow, and no one knew why they had gone hungry for so long. Your *zek*, now, he'll demand what's his even if he has to slit his own throat. Your warder, he'll steal it on the sly, so where's a serviceman to find his cut? You can't exactly weigh what comes in from the regiment. They say that the supplies meet regulations, but which regulations? Who knows? They ration by gross weight, as though they don't understand that grain settles out, or shrinks when cooked, or generally just vanishes away. Instead of proper nourishment, just that dreadful army margarine. And the fat is like water: you'll never feel full, and your very soul is repulsed by it. Instead of apples: dried fruit. They substitute this hot, tarry, tea-like concoction for actual tea. No matter where you look, they're scrimping and saving. Put plainly, the men weren't serving so much as surviving the best they could; and if you did manage to stuff yourself full, then for some reason you'd lose all your will to live.

The captain never let slip a word of complaint about his fate. Complaining meant picking someone to blame or evading responsibility, and these were things he did not know how to do. When he'd ended up in the sentry company, Khabarov had soon understood that there was no real military service here. There was just the same misery for everyone, the same toil: hauling this barge of a camp and all who sailed upon her, all struggling to keep down a rising seasickness. This was why he didn't like the camp commanders and had no respect for the peripatetic courts, when gawpers would crowd into the club building and sentences would be passed, even when for once the guilty copped it. This was a misfortune, and as at funerals, only those nearest and dearest should be present. A solitary individual shouldn't be held up for display and abuse. Khabarov plodded along under the camp's yoke, making life easier neither for himself, nor for the *zeks*, nor for the soldiers. Each man served out his time in the camp, but there, where they would only have died alone, they lived en masse, kept on their feet by being crammed together so tightly that not even a dead man could fall.

Only in winter did a sleepy silence hang heavy over the settlement, and a grimy off-white calm seep through, sending Karabas into hibernation. Throughout this long period, you could remember how life had abated, and the remembered warmth would heat you like a stove. The captain liked to drift away in this heat, which also soothed the sting of his many snubs and setbacks.

If it were possible, now that we have painted this picture of the camp settlement's expanse, to turn from the height we have already attained to its depths, then we'd have to fall like a stone into the barracks square, striking the eternally drunk Ilya Peregud, a man so huge that even without taking aim you would always hit.

Ilya Peregud served in the company in all the unfilled posts – those insignificant, transient jobs that won't make a man a commanding officer, but burden him with the mundane chores: counting the sheets in the stores, making sure the dogs have been fed. Karabas suffered from a permanent shortage of personnel, so all these duties fell to Peregud. He had first caught the captain's eye as a prison warder, being quite lost in that position. The captain had led him by the hand, like a little orphan child, across into his company. Ilya's heart and soul ran on vodka. Mind you, he wasn't keen on moving; he was usually to be found, like a bear in his den, at one of his posts, more often than not in the stores. Peregud would be located in a dark box room, which space he filled completely: a veritable coffin. Going in, a person would take Ilya for a dead man: he'd be sat there, his huge head with the topknot apparently ready at any moment to tumble off his great mound of a torso. One arm of this mighty warrior would rise into the air like a mountainside, and in the gloom a glugging noise would be heard, and then Ilya, sighing with relief after quenching his thirst. 'Just who are you? Are you a Cossack?' Peregud would ask pointedly, failing to recognise who had walked in. And then he'd answer himself, 'Well, I am a Cossack!'

It scarcely needs saying that Peregud didn't do a bloody thing about any of his duties. There was nothing he was able to do, in fact, apart from inspire respect. The dogs were not fed, the sheets not counted. But the disorder that reigned on his account throughout the company made life the merrier for everyone; they used to love taking the piss out of him. He was, in fact, an unrivalled source of entertainment. Peregud had never once in his life hit anyone, for fear of killing them. If they wound him up too much, he would just bellow in warning, 'You dare take the piss out of me? Out of a Cossack?' Or he would glower and get angry. He might punch a hole in something – one of the walls, maybe – in front of them and instantly regain their respect. From time to time, though, he would be seized by fear, as other people sometimes get aches in their bones before it rains. Once it happened that during one of these episodes someone whispered to Peregud that a patrol wagon was after him. So Ilya went and climbed under the cots in the barracks, and the soldiers deliberately kept him scared: 'You lay there, maybe they won't find you.' And there he lay, not moving, thinking it was all true. Then he was dragged out from under the bunks by the deputy political officer, Vasil Velichko, a man who always spoke the truth and stood up for the unfortunate.

As regards Vasil Velichko, the men themselves would tell you he was the sort of man who held nothing back and kept no secrets. This is the man we should have started with, in fact, if only Peregud hadn't turned up. Peregud could have waited, he wouldn't have gone anywhere, and he'd put up with anything so long as you poured vodka into his heart. But just you try and move past him!

If they had said to Captain Khabarov that Peregud had hidden himself under the cots, a stunt the soldiers had scared him into trying, he wouldn't even have stood up, let alone drop the matters that he was busy with. But Velichko, now, Velichko rushed off, all aflutter. That was the kind of man he was; he wanted to save everyone and change everything on earth!

It was easy to fall into Karabas, as easy as falling down a hole; but it was hard, to put it bluntly, to get out again. Never mind the *zeks*, even the soldiers were exiled, hidden deeper in the steppe, when they didn't pass muster at the regimental base. This Khabarov knew to be true, and when they had suddenly sent him a deputy political officer from the regiment, he had been scared that the newcomer would turn out to be completely beyond hope, one of those who had nothing to lose. On his very first day, Velichko organised a political-awareness class, sticking up some pretty good posters around the barracks, and daubing slogans there, too, although not many of the men understood what the slogans were exhorting them to do. The captain was even surprised by the meanness of the regimental commanders: why did they have to send a blessed fool like that away? They could have let him flutter about with his slogans at headquarters. Noting, later, that the company now had political classes and briefings, plus a cell of the Young Communist League, Khabarov grew depressed and muttered, 'This is all going to end badly.'

Every single story deputy political officer Velichko had about himself included the exclamation 'I became convinced', which was soon succeeded by 'I have overcome', but they all presented one and the same picture: he would start doing something, but then drop it as he got caught up in something else, and he would never see anything through to the end. According to his tales, he used to believe in God, but then lost his faith, and began practising body-temperature conditioning. 'I became convinced that a man can have control over himself, that he should be healthy and find joy in life!' Velichko exclaimed. And then, with the same feverishness, he took to recounting how he had lost faith in temperature conditioning when he understood that first you need to make everyone's life happy and joyful. 'I became convinced of this, it's the most important thing, do you understand? First we need to build communism! It's bad for a person when it's bad all around, but all together we can change the world!' The entire trajectory of Vasil Velichko's path through life was this: he had been getting by quietly in the service, but then he asked to transfer to the political department and be a propagandist, after which he was sent to serve in Karabas, probably so that nobody on earth would have to hear any more about him.

The soldiers loved their deputy political officer. Khabarov, he was alien. They feared him, or respected him. You could have a drink with Peregud, though it was like being with an old bloke. But Velichko brought posters and slogans with him, and from the very first days he hung out with the soldiers, even using the polite form of 'you' to them to start with, because the soldiers were the very people with whom he planned to change the world. Yet since he had to bring everyone round to his way of thinking, something special and sincere came about that would never have happened if he had set out to change everything by himself. If your stomach aches, go see Velichko, complain about it! If you want to pour your heart out, go see him, he'll listen all night, if need be! And while Khabarov still took the deputy political officer for a windbag, he began to treat him more gently, understanding that Velichko was genuinely trying his best on the men's behalf, never mind if his efforts brought little result. Anyway, could one man change everything?

A passionate dispute soon arose between Khabarov and Velichko, which bound them closer than any blood transfusion. The captain was forever putting things to one side for future use, and then eking out his stores for a long time. Even if there was enough of everything, he would still put something aside, expecting a plague, almost as though inviting disaster. The soldiers understandably grew downcast at these economies and lost all faith in the future. The deputy political officer was deeply troubled by this, and he would round on the captain whenever he tried to make a saving. Their silent battle, although it was certainly cantankerous at times, lasted for months, and it would have cost the captain nothing to overpower the fragile, dreamy political officer, but seeing his despair and pain, Khabarov surrendered. Peregud had popped up and made him laugh: 'Here, Ivan, give over with the starvation diet. The deputy political officer is right. Turn it around, you prick. Make all the cuts you want for yourself, but don't touch the men!' The system was shattered. Ivan Yakovlevich could hardly bear to look on as Velichko scattered his years of ant-like efforts to the wind for the sake of a single day's slackening of the reins. But seeing all this, he stayed submissively quiet. You would have thought that Vasil – and Peregud, for that matter – was a burden to him, and didn't provide the slightest assistance, but here's a funny thing: this burden made the captain's life cosier and his service easier.

No one admitted aloud that they needed anyone else, but the admission, albeit tacit, was there in the communal living arrangements made by this trio in the company's administrative office. Khabarov had moved in there ages ago. In Ugolpunkt – a little place not too far away, reached via the narrow-gauge line from Karabas – there was a separate brick-built hostel for the camp-workers in which it was possible to obtain a place to sleep. But the poky rooms there were shared between five, even for the family men. So the captain reckoned it would be more peaceful to live in his office. After Velichko had tried life with the camp warders and their unrefined families, he asked if the captain would let him have a billet. And then Ilya, when he had registered that the company commander and the deputy political officer were living right alongside him, followed a rule of staying at theirs as a guest every night. They billeted him on the floor, which suited him fine. After this, Khabarov was ashamed ever to think of driving him out again, which would be to deprive him of his pleasure, even if Ilya had decidedly impinged on their space and, what's more, afflicted them with conversations, the kind without beginning or end.

The air in the office became potent: as they breathed it, so they lived. Sometimes it would be Khabarov who hit the bottle, although you'd never believe he might go on a bender because, even when he drank, he did so stiffly, as though seeing someone off on a long journey. If he ever got drunk suddenly, all out of nowhere – and when he did, he would drink non-stop – it was only ever when a bit of gloomy time off, a veritable new dawn, turned up in his usual pointless routine. It was precisely during these peaceful times that, totting it all up, the captain would fancy there was no value to his life. When he was drunk, though, he didn't stagger around the company. He slept the sleep of the dead, which is to say he lay on his cot without even taking his boots off. Ilya would sleep on the floor by the captain's side like a dog, scaring away anyone who came in with his growl. Once a day, though, he would prod Ivan Yakovlevich to make sure that the captain was still alive.

Khabarov would need maybe a week to sleep it off, and then he would realise that the running of the place had been abandoned and would quit his drinking with ease.

Velichko was the only one who would have stayed teetotal. However, he too would sometimes start drinking, while attempting to re-educate Peregud, to turn him away from drunkenness. Peregud would promise, 'Enough. I swear. Not a drop, as my life depends on it. So come on, for the last time, let's share a glass together. Here, Vasiliok, listen, don't offend me. Drink to my new life!'

The deputy political officer would ask, 'Are you honestly going to stop drinking?'

'Cossack's honour, or don't you believe me?' Velichko would feel ashamed, and he hurriedly acquiesced, even though the vodka hit him like a truncheon, weakened as he was by the healthy lifestyle he'd been leading for so long.

Occasionally Velichko and Peregud would stage a mutiny, shouting, 'There's nothing for people to eat, there's no discipline left in the country, it's thief against thief!' Khabarov feared such conversations. He would suddenly interrupt: 'Quit going over the same old nonsense. We'd do better to have a drink. Let's have another little drink.' And he'd drink too. When he poured vodka on these troubled conversations, Khabarov more often than not exceeded his limits, and would again get extremely drunk all of a sudden. He would start to excoriate the authorities and the regulations so fiercely that Velichko and Ilya would turn pale, then red, and run out of the office like men possessed. In the end, Peregud would deliberately lay himself down to sleep on the floor and start snoring loudly: either he wanted to drown out the captain's tirades so that no one overheard him, or he was genuinely falling asleep, and this snoring was something that happened to him when he got scared in his sleep.

Khabarov could only set stuff aside from what was brought in. He could not siphon off a little something for himself, bypassing his superior officers – there was nothing to be had. Velichko complained more and more, and grew downcast. He used to dream about making everyone on earth happier, but he was driven to tears of torment by the fact that that he had caught lice in Karabas. He tried various scientific methods to rid himself of the parasites, but the lice would crawl back onto him straight away from the others.

One day, Velichko cancelled his political education class, saying, 'Forgive me, everyone, for lying to you all, because I raised questions then gave incorrect answers.' With something approaching joy, Khabarov replaced the political classes with domestic chores for the soldiers, who, mind you, got out of them easily, as ever. Seeing that no one appeared to be sorry about what had happened, Velichko felt his loneliness in Karabas even more acutely. Only the captain knew about the dispatch the deputy political officer had written in which he had requested to be discharged. However, a spiteful response came from somewhere, which was only to be expected. Five years was what he had left to serve, and he couldn't strip himself of his epaulettes, as according to the regulations this would make him a deserter.

A gunshot rang out in the office, followed by a long scuffling noise. The deputy political officer was found still alive. His eyes bulged. He was flapping his heavy-lipped mouth noiselessly. It was as if the bullet had nailed him to the floor. He had shot himself in the chest, much higher than the heart, as though he either did not really want to die or he did not know for sure where his heart actually was. As it was, his wound – just a little hole in his tunic – did not scare the men who had run in. The captain was late to appear in the office, when Velichko was already motionless, out cold on the floor. He was lying full length, and deathly quiet.

Ivan Yakovlevich ran for the camp, to demand assistance from the infirmary. He was gone for a long time: the *zeks* sector lived its own life, under its own officers and regulations. The military doctor who the captain tracked down, once he'd hurled twisted obscenities at everyone and everything to the extent that it was a wonder anyone could still understand him, got to work in an instant. The servicemen dispersed back to their sties, finding out over the course of that day that Vasil's life had been saved in the infirmary after all. The next morning, a vehicle arrived from the regiment, and only those who were loitering round the gatehouse, including Captain Khabarov, who happened to be passing by, got to see Velichko for the last time, as they were carrying him off.

There came rumours that Velichko had been recovering in the hospital, but they'd been curing him, it turned out, in order to pass sentence upon him. The head of the regiment's internal discipline enforcers – the 'Special Department' – arrived in Karabas, a man by the name of Smershevich. He was horrid in appearance: plump, fond of good food, and of drink. As well as this, though, he was hard, slab-like, with dark glinting eyes sunken in beneath his forehead. Eyes that, with his sour, forever dissatisfied expression, he would use unapologetically to transfix every man he met, as though seeing right through them. Everything about him made plain that people were worth nothing to him. He also had a crippled arm: a lonely false hand, covered in leather, did not quite conceal the stump of his right wrist. He wielded this false hand like a cudgel:

he'd wave it in the air or, far from attempting to shake your hand, he would thrust it right in your face. Actually, Smershevich did not know how to interrogate; no matter how much he huffed and puffed, he just brought all his backwardness to bear, pressing down with threats, hurling invective from all sides and tossing around tired old imprecations. 'Who are you covering for? That liar? That anti-Soviet element? I used to trip over him back at the regiment. That's when he should have been crushed!'

Khabarov remained silent, and Smershevich could not do anything with the captain. However, he fixed Khabarov in his mind and parted thus: 'You maggot, you'll see, you'll make quite a stink when they crush you.'

Afterwards, there was a hearing at the regiment where Vasil Velichko, already demoted and maimed for life, was expelled from the Party and sentenced to imprisonment by his peers. They also demanded the steppe captain's presence at the court, so that they'd know in Karabas, too, what punishment could be meted out for refusing to serve the motherland. Khabarov did not go. For the first time in his life, he did not follow an order. However, nothing came of it. Maybe they had only demanded it of him to tick a box. Maybe they'd decided that he too should suffocate in that dead end of his.

The regiment begrudged sending out a fresh person to replace Velichko. They raised Khabarov's own pay by a kopeck so he could take on Velichko's duties. So the captain, as though by some cruel joke, stepped up a rank, appointed to be his own personal deputy political

officer. This duty depressed him: scarcely a day went by
when Velichko didn't come into his mind. And then, too,
Peregud began to be tormented by panic attacks: he shut
himself up in his storeroom and rarely went outside. So
Ivan Yakovlevich Khabarov was left completely alone.

The captain had several years to go before retirement. At
one time, he had been cheered by the thought that he
had such a short time left to serve. Moving through the
years towards his pension, it was as if Ivan Yakovlevich
knew what he had to live for. However, it had been a
long time since he had had anywhere to go back to after
the army. The captain was lodged in the administrative
office and he also boarded in the barracks, eating from
the same pot as the soldiers. He had grown used to this.
Knowing that, one day very soon, they would cross him
off the list of those entitled to allowances and boot him
out onto the steppe, Khabarov was still waiting for his
pension, albeit with the fanciful belief that he would have
at least a month of the rest he deserved; they would let
him occupy the office for a month or so more, he would
catch up on his sleep, he would lie in, take a deep breath,
and then he would die painlessly in his sleep.

Thinking over his personal demise, Khabarov began
making assumptions about a lot of things in advance.
'We'll live the way we always have,' he said repeatedly,
in a tired voice, when the regimental supply truck turned
up, complaining only that once again they'd been a bit

stingy over how many potatoes they had sent. 'Well, there's enough here for us not to die, but tell me, lads, what are we going to live on?' Nobody knew any longer why this sickening, harsh life was happening, as though it were being meted out by a troubled conscience. The events that were transforming everything in the world did not make it as far as the steppe – they got lost on the way. This was why, to the servicemen, the very journey from this forsaken settlement to Karaganda seemed longer than a lifetime. And although it was an ordinary truck that made this journey to the settlement, the soldiers crowded round its driver – rendered inert by the jolting – as though he were a guest from overseas. But the fiend would not stick around in the community: as soon as he had unloaded, he was off. They only saw him fleetingly, in fact. He had brought rotten potatoes, which made the captain ponder. 'That means the regiment is only getting sent rotten supplies, too.'

He was not worried for himself; he was retiring soon, after all. However, Khabarov would have been easier in his mind if he could have been sure he was at least of some value to people. Meanwhile, the rotten portion of what the regiment had sent them – very nearly half the delivery – they buried a good distance off, so as not to smell it. There's no telling how much was buried, perhaps an entire collective farm's worth; but in that obscure year, at the edge of one of these dumping grounds out in the steppe, thickly overgrown with wormwood, the tops of a potato plant broke through. One hungry soldier noticed them, and dug them up in search of the tubers at the roots, still green. This came to light by chance. The soldier ate the tiny potatoes there and then, raw. A bit later, he had stomach cramps. They tried to figure out what was wrong with him. He told the captain about the potatoes, but Khabarov did not believe him, deciding that the soldier must have secretly stuffed himself with soil, and was now feigning food poisoning. The poor lad writhed in pain, and threw up some gluey, porridge-like substance. They laughed at him, but then, after all, the potato tops were found. They reconsidered their opinion of the soldier's honesty, and the captain was like a new man.

Khabarov decided to visit this site in the steppe. He sat down on a little rise, breathed in the wormwood and looked off into the hollow, deserted distance. And the following thought came to him: what if, come the spring, we make a vegetable plot in the steppe? We could plant potatoes, too. From one potato, so they say, you can get a whole bucketful. We'll barter potatoes for meat from the Kazakhs, and then, when the company has got rich on potatoes, we'll get our own livestock. Perhaps they won't drive me into retirement. Perhaps they'll let me stay around the smallholding, if it turns out to be useful. He would supply the regiment with potatoes and meat. And so Ivan Yakovlevich decided that he would wait for the next delivery. He would plant all the potatoes they were allotted. Meanwhile, they would live on grains and boiled-down beef suet until the plants grew. They'd get by.

2

POTATOES

The flies, snakes and birds that had disappeared, some in the autumn, some in the winter, had not yet reappeared. So life was sad in the early spring, as the only remaining living things were in fact men and lice. These latter creatures, which you cannot catch, or even spot, began to reveal their true nature: as soon as a man was starving, without hope, they would begin multiplying on him in their myriads, making themselves just as unfed and unhopeful. Dejection was omnipresent in the community. Even the air inside had irrevocably spoiled and was swarming with lice. That is, it too was, in a way, quick on the uptake and liable to move by itself.

On that first day, after the potatoes had been trucked in to Karabas, the captain held the men back. He baffled the poor lads with some nonsense about the need to sort through the potatoes to decide which were good and how many to allot to each man's ration. As they sorted through, the servicemen ate on the sly, even though the potatoes were raw – having got frozen in transit, they were crumbly and sweet. The captain did not make a fuss. He calculated that they would not take many away, counting on the rations to come, and that they wouldn't even start hiding them.

That night, Khabarov was scared to fall asleep. Hungry mice scoured the office, gnawing at – or, at any rate, trying their teeth on – all the crude fixtures it contained. Time melted slowly away, and the captain's resolve faltered as he felt the early morning cold. For the rest of the night, he wavered on the point of changing his mind: the soldiers would refuse to dig the vegetable plot, and if they did not get their appointed rations, they would burn down the barracks. And so the captain got up while it was still half-dark and sat at the small window. The heavens brightened before his eyes, opening their vaults while the endless shoals of the steppe emerged from the gloom.

His heart-rending voice, sounding almost drunk, rang out through the sleeping barracks. Once he had sounded the battle alarm, the captain armed the soldiers with entrenching tools and drove them from the bright, dead square into the steppe. Gasping for breath, the soldiers whispered to each other, 'Where is he taking us? The pisshead, what's got into him?' The captain meanwhile had taken to waving his arms about, as though giving commands on the battlefield. The soldiers launched an attack on the great expanse of empty land, and dug it over, following Khabarov's directions. The captain staggered along the creeping ranks, brandishing his pistol whenever the digging stopped without permission, and offering encouragement: 'Keep those shovels working!' The amount of dug-over soil grew ever bigger. He measured it out with an unwavering stride until he ran out of steam, at which point he ordered them all to line up along the edge of the field. The sacks were brought out in front of the ranks, who stood rigid, and then shouts rang out: 'Brothers, look! That's our grub he wants to bury in the ground!' Khabarov tried to drown out these howls with a shout that cracked with despair: 'Silence! It's not our rations we're burying in the ground, it's our future. In half a year you'll be eating mashed potato by the bucketload!' But the loudest mouths in the unit ran out in front and started yelling at the tops of their voices, 'Brothers! We refuse! These are our rations!' Khabarov tried to convince them: 'They'll grow by themselves, there's no need to put any effort into them . . . I'm doing this for you, I want to make sure there will be something to live on in future . . . ' But they shouted him down, roaring, 'We refuse! We've heard enough about life! Company commander, let us eat!'

Then the captain scattered whatever was left of the potatoes, and began planting the tubers into the earth himself. Clocking his pistol, the soldiers did not dare attack, although that awesome weapon did not save the captain from the deluge of invective and clods of earth they were hurling, beyond fear. Yet he was glad: they had dug over the earth; he could never have turned over so much soil by himself. Knowing he was guilty of a deception, he did not try to avoid the clods of earth. He quickly hid the potatoes in the plot, covering them over.

The crowd dispersed. After spending the whole day alone in the field, Khabarov considered his return to the barracks despondently. However, the company positions turned out to be quiet. They either did not acknowledge the captain, or skirted past him sullenly. Still, there was one man who snorted, 'You should sleep, boss, you must be tired.'

The captain awoke late in the morning, thinking that the servicemen had forgiven him completely and performed the company reveille themselves. When he had washed, he stepped into the cookhouse, where he did find some soldiers. A significant aroma of fried potatoes struck out from the kitchen at his belly. 'Where's that coming from?' he said, in surprise. A merry little cook leaned through the serving hatch, its shutters open. His frying pans were still sizzling. 'Ta-dah! Scoff as much as you want!'

In a daze, Khabarov ran to the field. His potatoes lay scattered along the paths in the square. That was why no riots had started! By now the captain was crawling along the ground, gathering the remaining ones. The soldiers probably hadn't bothered to drag these off, which was why they were scattered about like pebbles.

When he made it back to the barracks, the first soldier he met – lounging at the gateway, lazily puffing on a greasy cigarette – choked on his smoke when he recognised this crooked, filthy individual, dragging a sack that looked like it was crammed with stones along the ground, as his captain.

The servicemen had stuffed themselves to their hearts' content on fried food. They were exhausted. They were having a quiet afternoon nap. Forgotten, Khabarov yelled, in an alien tone, 'Get up! Where's the rest? Where? You can't have eaten them all . . . Listen, I'll give you no rest, you bastards, not one of you!' The barracks barely stirred.

'Put a sock in it, we've heard that song before.'

'Brothers, really, what's he on about now?'

'Listen, Khabarov, we're gonna write to the prosecutor, and that's the truth!'

'Yeah, yeah, cap'n. Ransack the place. What you find is yours. Or piss off, and don't rain on our parade.'

'Yeah . . . And if you start waving your gat around, we'll see you off ourselves. Just try touching it, everyone will sign a statement!'

'What's this then? It's my death you want?' sighed Khabarov, at this. 'I'll tell you this: you'll return those potatoes. You'll plant them back in the ground with your own hands, to the very last one. If you refuse, you bunch of pricks, come evening roll-call I'll shoot myself right before your very eyes.'

He shut up, and sighed again with annoyance, looking round at the men, who had grown quiet. He had spoken out recklessly in his anger. As he cooled off, Captain Khabarov understood that he had sentenced himself to death; he went limp, as though all his bones had melted, and dragged himself away to his poky little room in the office.

The barracks resembled a cowshed, being so extended and driven so deeply into the ground that the roof practically buried the rooms beneath it. Indoors, it was cramped from the sides, while the ceiling pressed down from above. A corridor, just as oppressive as the exterior walls, ran along it, onto which opened the doors of all the barrack rooms. There was even regimentation in the barracks, but of a particular, unaccommodating kind: iron bunks, fairly screwed into the floors, and bare walls.

It was along this corridor, in its emptiness, that Khabarov was dragging himself to his office. It occurred to him that dying would be painful. It also occurred to him that there would be a mere emptiness left in his place. People had lived before him, had shared their blood for him, but he would just spill that blood into a black quagmire. He was such a useless person that truly the best thing for him to do would be to die.

Oblivious to the world, Khabarov lay down on his bunk. He forced himself to stay on the bunk and pretend to be asleep, intent on staying put instead of running out to his men. Outside, it was getting dark. Voices called out, increasingly faint, fading into the evening hush. The need to piss seized the captain; it was unbearable. There was a little pail in the office, a veritable slop bucket. He screwed up his eyes in shame, and relieved himself in the pitch dark. And trembled for fear they would hear him.

When they knocked on the door, he decided to pretend to be asleep. They worked the door frame over harder, and it began to crack. 'Comrade Captain? Boss? Are you still alive?' And Khabarov let slip, 'Here I am . . . ' A happy noise went up the other side of the door. 'Well, we've returned the potatoes for you! Just like you said, right back in the ground, there. We, well, we decided to live in peace with you, meaning we pulled in a few favours. Nuff said.'

Khabarov opened the door to the petitioners. They were struck dumb, fixing their eyes on his feet, which were bare, and turning blue. 'Looks like I'm still alive.'

The soldiers shuffled their feet, hesitating. 'Er, just so as you know, we kept just a few of the spuds back. Did we ought to replant them?' And the captain said, 'Eat them, but I won't allow it again.'

So that the plot was not ransacked again, the captain chained up two strong guard dogs at its edges. Their viciousness and their resounding barks ought to have done the trick. Come the morning, the field was empty: all trace of the dogs had vanished and the patch had once again been dug up. The feasting held by the soldiers that night spread furtively through the barracks. It was only by the appetising smells that Khabarov worked out they had fried some meat and were eating it, with a side dish of potatoes. They had killed the guard dogs and, once they were skinned, the soldiers had fried and eaten them, as if unsentimentally disposing of something that had outlived its usefulness.

The ones who had feasted were identifiable by their swollen stomachs. Khabarov kicked a good half of the company out onto the steppe and ordered them not to come back. Once they had roamed around the district, frozen and starving, these gourmets returned all the same, demanding their lawful ration. There was nowhere for them to run. They gave their solemn word that henceforth they would not steal from the field.

Many of them kept their word. They restrained themselves and even helped look after the field. They surrounded it with barbed wire, which lay about the place rusting uselessly in huge coils. But many others conceived a hatred of this field. Still, the potatoes managed to grow, and so there came to be more and more doubters in the company: sure, it's a pity about the rations, but it would be a pity too to crush the shoots, now that they're out; let whatever comes, come.

The dry steppe summer flared up. The earth around the potato field was cool. The servicemen went there in crowds, seeking escape from the dejection and the heat. And the *zeks* clambered onto the barracks roofs and perched as high as they could within the confines of their zone, gazing at the luxuriant green plant tops, seeming to see in them some far-off, wondrous gardens. Occupying the roofs was forbidden by the regime, but driving the prisoners down from there would have been tantamount to forbidding birds from flying in the heavens. It angered the *zeks* that their guards would even set barbed wire around an unfettered patch of steppe. Now and then the natural sounds of the steppe would be drowned out by yells from the rooftops:

'One zone's not enough for you, you want to put everything in harness!'

'Come out of there, you, take the harness off, if you dare!'

'If ever we meet outside, you won't have time to know about it, you dog!'

'You should plant your own potatoes, there's plenty of land!'

'You don't get fat if the soup's like dishwater!'

'So drink your dishwater, then!'

'And you choke down your bastard rations!'

'That's you lot: not thieves, but bastards!' And then the wound-up, nervous bosses would come running out from each side at the double, while the soldiers and the *zeks* vanished in a flash.

The camp commandant, Vilor Sinebriukhov, and the company captain usually avoided each other. Sinebriukhov had been in charge at the camp for many years, so that by comparison Khabarov's residency in Karabas appeared merely transient. However, through all the time that they had been fated to serve in the same place, these two commanders had not grown neighbourly. If they came together by some chance, they would look at each other with such surprise that in other contexts it would have been offensive, and of their own accord would go their separate ways. 'What an idiot, and still at liberty,' the camp commandant would say, with Khabarov in mind.

The captain in turn would express surprise: 'I can't believe the ground can still bear to hold him up!'

'Good spuds, them, right enough!' Sinebriukhov smacked his lips as he looked at the potato field. 'They'd go nicely with a little lightly salted herring, ah, a drop of vodka and a bit of black bread . . . Some people set up a vegetable plot and other people have to sort it all out; the workload increases for the other people in the camp.'

'Oh, no, you'd choke on them. You're not going to steal this away, this isn't your little factory in the camp we're talking about, you thieving bastard,' in his head, Khabarov swore at him. 'People like you should be locked up.'

The potato field gave rise to genuine horror in the breast of Ilya Peregud. He was a man who feared anything that appeared to change, anything that was being constructed or even anything that grew. He became scared and complained tiresomely to Khabarov. 'That's it. We'll all die here, I can tell. What have you gone and done? They'll eat us alive, the wolves . . . I know it for sure . . . '

The potatoes bloomed. With the potatoes in flower, Khabarov went picking this simple beauty. He arranged the flowers in tin mugs throughout the barracks, as though they were long-awaited messages from the earth. The men took them on the sly, and tried them, putting them in their mouths and then spitting them out, sharing their conclusions: 'Do they smell of anything?'

'No, like water. You chew them, they're ever so tart.'

They began to undermine the potatoes. Khabarov guarded the field at night. He felt sorry for his potatoes.

And he was scared: what was going to happen in the future? To keep up his morale, he affirmed to himself: 'I am a captain. That's the single most combat-effective unit.'

Khabarov soon got the knack of hunting for people in the potato field. Every night he would wait among the potato tops, not for a person ready to flee, but for an enemy. One time he captured a Kalmyk on the field, one of his own soldiers. The captain walloped him, pressing his forehead down into the earth so that he did not squirm, and went through his clothes, shaking out the tiny, pea-sized potatoes. He started dragging the Kalmyk by the hair, like so much dead meat, to eject him from the field. Suddenly, Khabarov grew perplexed, realising that you cannot cultivate ruined potatoes, you cannot plant them back. At this, his anger lost its strength. Weakening, the captain wondered, 'So why am I killing people? A man has nothing apart from his life and here I am taking that away from him!' He raised the Kalmyk and carried him, not knowing where he should drag him to, but wanting only for the other man's situation to improve.

Afterwards, if he pounced on people, it was only with the potato patches in mind, so that they would not get trampled. Any people he found were now silently chased away. Sometimes he would yell into the night, 'Let them draw strength, let them grow! Wait! Have some pity!' And it would happen that these unexpected calls in the night shook even the most cold-blooded soldiers by their very unexpectedness, so that they lost their heads and would reply, 'We're not up to anything, we're just taking a stroll by the field!'

When the sunny days and summer blooms came to an end, the rains gave the earth no respite. It became charred and heavy, like a fire that has been quenched. The birds feared to fly in such weather, and roamed across the damp earth with bowed heads. In between the downpours, they flew off to warmer climes, flapping their damp wings heavily, as if they were cast-iron.

Worry oppressed Khabarov, too. When the sun blazed, he was happy, thinking that the potatoes were absorbing its warmth. And when the rains poured, he was happy, thinking that the potatoes were drinking their fill. However, the captain did not know when to dig up the potatoes, as if this had to happen on a single day, like death or birth.

In the company office, the electric light shone feebly; they were definitely cutting down the supply. Mice roamed the floor heedless of Khabarov, although they were squeaking about something in very fearful, complaining tones. The captain had never believed in God, but he suddenly got down on his knees in the middle of the office. He called out to him loudly. And he did not pray, mind, he did not bow down, never having known how to; rather he held himself upright, like an honest soldier on parade. To begin with, he reported that throughout this great country there was nothing but rotten potatoes. And after he had fallen silent and brought his breathing under control, he asked, 'If You actually exist, then help my company, if possible, to gather plenty of potatoes. For this, I will start to believe in You, and I will pay with my life, if that is required.'

Maybe it was the mice scratching and rustling, but it seemed to the captain that a whisper, ever so quiet, ran through the office, so that even his breath caught at the unexpected compassion. Khabarov felt deeply sorry for himself in the holy silence that suddenly surrounded him. He did not hear anything more, as though he had gone deaf. But when he noticed the first rays of dawn glimmering in the window, he marched into the barracks to rouse the soldiers.

He awoke them one by one, persuading each to get up: 'Get up, son, help me this one last time, you see I haven't got anyone else.' The servicemen forced themselves out of their bunks.

When they got to the field, the company waited for the fog to clear. In silent torment, the captain looked over the potato patches and the equally earthy, sullen faces of the soldiers. 'Right, well, put your backs into it . . . ' He waved his hand, sending them off through the pre-dawn silence along the dimly lit edges of the field.

The spades' sudden incursion stirred the motionless breast of the earth. A metallic grinding and ringing clove through the chilly silence, which shattered under their weight, sending a wave of pitiful cold into the men's hearts. You had only to turn over the patches for potatoes to pour out. The soldiers did not have hands enough to gather and stuff them into sacks. Flushed by such a victory, the captain wandered off to one side, away from everyone. Soldiers were already dragging sacks of potatoes back to the barracks, as though they were fallen comrades.

Then they washed their blackened hands in silence, apart from the sound of running water. They cast off their overalls, sticky with mud, and everyone was issued with clean underwear. Barefoot, in just their vests and pants, they sat at the trestle tables like dummies, no longer feeling either hungry or cold. Orders came to fry the potatoes, which still smelt of soil, and also, due to a lack of frying pans, to boil them in cauldrons and dress them with melted fat. Later, when it was already getting on for night-time, the dinner was served. The potatoes, still steaming, were devoured by buzzing mouths.

To set the seal on the day, the captain was supposed to ring the regiment and give his usual short report. The report was received by the officers on duty at the regiment, who rarely passed on anything in return themselves, unless they were known to Khabarov. The communication link went something like this: first, you ring the regiment and request a conversation; only then do they provide one, as they see fit.

The telephone was black and heavy, the receiver flattened by two weighty fists; it had a strict, official air. Peregud, whose drinking had made him a superstitious man, seriously believed that this telephone was used to eavesdrop on all the conversations that took place in the office, and for this reason he hardly ever swore there.

Captain Khabarov himself sometimes felt tormented when he caught sight of the phone, although the apparatus looked lifeless.

The time for this mandatory call had long since passed. It was surprising to think that someone at the regiment might have given Karabas its liberty. Mind you, Khabarov would have liked to conceal everything. The potatoes had been grown from the regimental supplies and so still needed to be accounted for; they were property of the state. It had been easy to hide them in the ground, but now it did not seem right. He had become hopelessly confused, to the point of exhaustion. And then the telephone suddenly began to rumble in the office, blowing out sonorous bubbles.

The ringing did not abate, but bubbled on, giving the captain such bad shakes that he was almost fizzing. No longer able to endure this torture, he tore the receiver from the hook and heard the old-woman's babble of the switchboard operator: 'Calling the Sixth, calling the Sixth, come in, comrade Khabarov! . . . Khabarov? Wait, I'm connecting you, there's someone to speak to you.'

Something crackled and strange voices burst in, but soon a deep, powerful silence flowed along the line. Immobile, bewildered, the captain waited a good half-hour. At one point he tried to blow down the receiver that had apparently gone dead, and knocked it, to check whether it had indeed broken, but he was pulled up by a distant voice. 'Stop blowing, comrade Khabarov. Have you not realised who you're about to speak to? You can wait!' Matters had taken a strange, not to say mysterious, turn. The captain suddenly realised that actually he did not understand anything. Something had occurred, the likes of which had never happened before. Then he was told from afar, 'He's still busy. Keep waiting.'

The captain was overcome by chills, as though he had been stripped naked and presented for someone's close inspection. And then the silence was broken: he was shaken by a voice that was more than powerful. 'Khabarov?'

'Yes, sir. Captain Khabarov.'

'I already know you're a captain. So, what? Are you still asleep?'

'No, sir! I am on duty!'

'You see? He's on duty! So what's all this business with the potatoes you've got going on there? Bloody hell!'

In a daze, the captain blurted out: 'Permission to report, sir! The potatoes! They are all in one piece, so they are!'

'Ach, in one piece, eh? But how come they're there at all, with no orders? What are you up to? Who do you think you are, the regimental commander?'

'Yes, sir . . . No, sir . . . I was too scared to report it . . . Permission to report, sir . . . ' spewed out Khabarov. The voice cut in, loftily: 'You're lying. I know your brother – if he's not a thief, he's an idiot. Whose potatoes are they now? Eh? How many are there now? What were you thinking? Answer me!'

'To feed the men.'

'You what? How can that be?'

'The soldiers are living on just grains. We get supplied rotten food. You can't buy anything for money, you see, the army stores don't make it out this far! It's like we're not alive out here, or something!' erupted Khabarov.

'And did you report this to the regimental commander?'

'No, sir!'

'So that's how it is! Utter chaos, and they put up with it, they don't say a word. Is that really a regiment? It's a pile of shit! Well, I don't know. They're dying of hunger, how can it have come to this? It's all clear to me now. Well done, captain. Potatoes, were you saying? Well, then, it's in the nick of time. I'll support you in this.'

'Yes, sir! We should set up a smallholding! There's plenty of land, here. It could help us out, and other people, too. We could have everything we need right here: meat and veg, too.'

'How do you mean? So that you'd feed yourselves?' The voice thawed with understanding. 'That's the right solution. That's right, so long as, you understand, you put everything in their mouths! I support this, yes . . . There's plenty of land, here, you're thinking along the right lines, with that. It's everywhere around us, that's right, the land is. You see? You've put some thought into this! Well done!'

'Someone needs to give me the orders, though!' Khabarov dared to slip a word in. 'The orders! It's just that I'm due to retire, I'm worried I might not have time . . . '

The voice was outraged. 'What now? Let a fellow like you go? I won't allow it! Like it or not, you'll be serving 'til your dying day. You'll get your orders! I've found out all there is to know about you. Just wait. I'll turn this regiment over from top to bottom, I'll have them run off their feet! The dirty, filthy, you know, pieces of shit!' The receiver buzzed, and then that powerful silence flowed out once again.

The switchboard operator's babble cut in, bringing the captain back down to earth. 'Come in the Sixth. There will be no further communication, I am disconnecting you.'

Khabarov held the receiver in his hands for a long time before he replaced it. He had not even noticed that scared faces were being thrust into the office, that the door had long since stood wide open and the soldiers had gathered on the threshold as though on parade, and were eavesdropping and peeking in at what was happening. 'So who were you talking to?' He turned around quietly, surprised to see them, and the words came from him of their own accord: 'To a general . . . ' It seemed to surprise the captain that they believed him without a sound. Actually, he'd meant to say, 'Probably to a general . . . ' But now he himself believed that he had been talking to a general. Who else could it have been? The soldiers went quiet; their envious glances scorched him.

'Well, my lads, now you'll get enough to eat. We'll be feeding us, ourselves. We'll have everything we need to live on. Everything!' said the captain, joyfully. 'All I've got to do now is wait for the orders . . . Wait, just wait, now.'

However, no one cheered up. The soldiers began to disperse quietly. Meanwhile, the captain spent the rest of the night babysitting the potatoes. They were piling the sacks into a clapboard shack where they housed the dogs over winter. All the written-off equipment – broken pails or worn-through boots – was dumped in this shack, where it grew into great clumps. The shack had an electric lightbulb and a strong padlock, which between them were worth more than all the rubbish stored within.

The captain stumbled and bashed his head, regretting the absence of a decent store for his potatoes. It made him angry, he vowed to ring and report it . . . The soldiers were shifting the potatoes in. The captain dragged the sacks around, so that they formed an ordered rank, even putting right the ones that were already in place, as if he was scared to be found with nothing to do. Then, when he was left by himself in the little shack, he poured a few sacks' worth into a pile and began to sort the potatoes into large and small: he left the smaller ones for food, but he put the very heaviest and healthiest-looking tubers to one side, already dreaming about growing more like these.

Forcing himself to sort through the potatoes diligently, Khabarov soon became worn out. They were falling from his hands and his failing eyesight could scarcely tell big from small as he slipped into a doze. When he finally sank into his bunk, his body, like that of a stranger, fell straight asleep. But his head was already anxiously contemplating the company farm.

3

COMRADE SKRIPITSYN

One boring morning, dull as the reflection in a puddle of rainwater, a regimental lorry scraped along the full length of the clumsy gate and wobbled its way into the barrack square, where it stood snarling or belching, one of the two. Its canvas belly was empty, but it had grown heavy from being jolted across the trackless steppe. In the square, dragging on a soggy cigarette, was a sentry: a young Tatar boy with a drooping lip to which the cigarette had stuck, wreathing his unwashed face with white smoke. He half-rose, squinting at the lorry while dragging harder on his expiring dog-end. In just his underwear, wearing his boots without socks, the Tatar boy tried to give the vehicle standing by the gatehouse a cunning once-over. This arrival had been accompanied by a most unusual hush. The guard dogs had stayed quiet, although usually brutish howls erupted from Karabas as soon as they caught a whiff of strangers. And so the Tatar boy looked on as if it were merely smoke, which was the only reason he didn't get scared when out of the smoke – that is, out of the truck – some people emerged.

The first he made out to be a real fine specimen, one of those healthy and strong Russian soldiers who serve the officer class separately. The one who emerged after this paragon, however, was not an officer at all, but a specialist warrant officer in swamp-green epaulettes. His greatcoat did not improve this person's appearance; in fact it laid bare all his awkwardness; it hung from his rounded shoulders and, where it should have concealed his rear end, his backside drew the material taut and, incredibly, like a mountain, thrust itself out. Meanwhile, his chest and paunch wobbled. The man himself was at best average in height, so the hems of his greatcoat almost swept the floor.

'Where has everyone gone?' shrieked the warrant officer, alarmed.

'They're asleep,' said the Tatar lad, rubbing his hands in the chilly wind.

'What about your captain? Where's Khabarov?'

'He's asleep. Everyone's asleep.'

'Here, you. You . . . why aren't you saluting a senior rank?'

'No one salutes here, that's the sort of people we've got.'

'What sort of nonsense is this?' the warrant officer grumbled. 'Just where did that old blockhead ring?' He looked at the Tatar boy with both curiosity and disgust, as he might look at a louse he'd caught. The new arrival was tired, and his weak, constricted voice almost made him seem kind, even if he was looking both round about and directly at the Tatar lad with no warmth whatsoever. It was clear he'd spent more than just the one day travelling: the grey cloth of his greatcoat was covered in dust from the road. He couldn't stand still, so set off walking about the empty, slushy square. The young Tatar latched on to him, splashing after him through the mud. 'Who are you, anyway, what have you come to us for? Have you been posted here?' The warrant officer did not respond to these questions, as though he hadn't even heard them. Instead, he sought some answers of his own. 'So, just what's really going on here?'

'I don't know, truth be told,' said the Tatar lad, in surprise. 'We haven't got anything here.'

'But why is everyone asleep?'

'I don't know. I don't give a toss about 'em. I like being on my own.'

'Are there any other officers in the company, aside from Khabarov?'

'I don't know who there is or who there isn't. There was Velichko, the deputy political officer, but he's gone, banged up in the zone. There's Peregud, but he'll be sleeping off the booze. I don't know where. Maybe he's around, maybe not. And Khabarov's asleep, so they won't wake him. Here, listen to this! Yesterday, a general rang him. They reckon that Khabarov will go away soon, the general will take him. So, what about you, then? Are you our new commander?' The warrant officer kept quiet, and the Tatar boy took umbrage, deciding that they didn't believe him. 'He did! Everyone heard it. Cross my heart. The general himself rang!'

By now, as he looked around the deserted yard, the warrant officer was sure that he hadn't been expected and no one had made ready to meet him. Increasingly irritated, he tore into the bright specimen still waiting idly by the truck. 'Sanka, quit standing there like an idiot!' This Sanka stepped smartly across, and stretched, scaring the Tatar off. The warrant officer did not lift his eyes from the ground and the lanky soldier waited obediently. 'You know what, Kolodin? I'm going to take a walk around. You keep your eyes on that shack there, don't let anyone near it. That's material evidence. And get the company up on their feet before I get back. Parade them in the square, and let them wait.'

The soldier said nothing in reply, because, most likely, he had been taught to carry out every order in silence as soon as his boss gave the word. The warrant officer walked around the clapboard shack that had caught his eye, and then around the barracks, too; he moved sluggishly, and looked into every window. When he had disappeared behind a distant corner, Kolodin turned towards the Tatar lad, but the boy let fly insolently at the newcomer: 'What you looking at, anyway? Give me a smoke!' Kolodin flourished his fist and punched him, and when the Tatar boy fell down, clapping his hands over his busted mouth, said to him indifferently, 'Get up . . .

Who's the company sentry? You heard, the order was to rouse them.' But the Tatar lad just rolled around in the doorway, moaning. 'Bastard! What did you do that for? You've knocked a tooth out. Ow!' Kolodin grabbed him and gave him a good shake. 'I said, who's on sentry?' In his anger he raised his hands again and the Tatar started snivelling even more wretchedly, his startled, scared eyes open wide to the bad weather. 'Go wash your ugly mug. And go wake up your "sort of people". You heard what was said. Tell them to go line up in the square.'

A short while later, the anxious soldiers were crowded in the square under Kolodin's watchful eye, while the Tatar, now washed and with all his buttons done up, sat nearby, at the entrance, inspiring envy as well as blind fury among the company. He was regally smoking a cigarette given to him by Kolodin, and between drags he would spit, trying to hit his fellow soldiers.

The soldiers dodged in silence, and only the very bravest showered obscenities upon him from afar. The company had tended to shun the Tatar, being somewhat afraid of the stupid stunts he used to pull, and now he had properly scared them all, waking the barracks up with bloodcurdling howls and proffering his knocked-out tooth for each of them to touch. 'There's some power for you! No one ever knocked me tooth out before, but he did.' The Tatar lad was still boasting now, and asking Kolodin for smokes: one cigarette after another. But once he'd got them, he jealously drove off anyone else who tried to join in getting a bit of baccy off the lad who'd just arrived. The

Tatar puffed himself up and hissed: 'These freebies – he knocked me tooth out, what did he do for you?'

'I won't give any more out, anyway,' responded Kolodin.

'That's right, Sasha, don't. I'll have 'em all. Do you know how much it hurt? 'Ere, look, this gap will be with me all me life.'

Remembering the gap, he went quiet, for no other reason than that he was delving about in it on the sly with his tongue, and tears again sprang unbidden to his eyes. He found it both insulting and painful. The Tatar simply couldn't come to terms with the loss of his tooth. He pulled out the little smoke-yellowed pebble from his pocket and again tried to stick it back in its burning socket.

No one noticed the warrant officer had returned, he appeared so noiselessly. He emerged from the opposite side, having circled around on the steppe. The crowd shook in confusion, people turned their heads, looking around, thinking they had stumbled into an ambush.

'Brothers!' someone yelled. 'That's Skripitsyn himself, he's a regimental investigator. Everyone at the regiment knows him. He's the one who shipped me off.' Kolodin instantly sprang up, acknowledging his boss. The Tatar lad once more struck fear into them when he leapt up and saluted; their breath caught, although they still did not salute the investigator. 'Comrade Skripitsyn!' A red-faced soldier singled himself out. 'I'm Prikhodko, you remember? You were interrogating me, I'd done over the stores?'

'No, I don't remember . . . '

'What do you mean? That was some interrogation, and you don't remember! Last year, this was. It was you who got me sent here, I did over the stores. Prikhodko, that's me . . . ' Skripitsyn remained silent and simply glared at him malevolently.

'Their captain's asleep,' Kolodin hastened to report. 'He's not waking up by himself, and I didn't want to order him woken up without you.'

'Good,' Skripitsyn cut in. 'I left my briefcase in the truck, bring it to me.'

The case that Sanka brought to his boss was entirely ordinary; it made the man seem a mediocre, dreary being. As badly scraped as though someone had gone at it with emery paper, its original firm shape long gone, the case had clearly been in service way past its allotted term, which gave it a sinister air. It resembled a trunk and seemed to have been refashioned to carry heavy weights rather than papers. Standing with it, somewhat elevated on the steps leading down from the gatehouse, even Skripitsyn instantly took on a new aspect. Something weighty and capacious appeared about both his stooping posture and his oar-like arms. Even now, he hardly looked at anyone directly, rather angling his drooping head and unblinking, motionless stare off to one side. When he did suddenly look straight at someone, he would catch them completely unaware, and then study them shamelessly with curiosity and disgust. His face appeared profoundly stupid, but also frightening. The case gave Skripitsyn the appearance of those medical orderlies posted to obscure military hospitals that are built like drying rooms or barracks who, if they treat you, will surely cripple you. And if they are walking about with briefcases, then the cases contain nothing but a selection of saws and hammers: blunt instruments.

'Make sure they don't run off, because they might feel the need,' he said to Sanka. 'And make sure they don't go near the shack. That, especially.'

Turning about with great difficulty, exactly as if tumbling over, Skripitsyn marched into the barracks and, without asking which direction to take, was soon lost in its depths, as though he were one of the company and knew the building inside out.

It was quiet behind the door of the company office, quieter than Skripitsyn's breathing. Establishing that the captain was indeed asleep, Skripitsyn knocked loudly, deliberately, so as to wake him, and did not stop.

There was nothing strange in the fact that he woke up a sleeping person by knocking, but Skripitsyn's actions made it look as though he were trying to break into the office. When he woke Khabarov, he must really have scared him, which was why the captain hurriedly flung open the door and appeared half-naked in the cold, while Skripitsyn, standing on the threshold in his greatcoat, took his time about coming in. Loitering, he prolonged this somehow significant pause, then at a stroke he crossed the threshold and was already in the middle of the office when he addressed the captain: 'It's cold in here; you should light the stove, seeing as you've taken up living here.'

Approaching the desk as though it were specially designed for him, Skripitsyn began to make himself at home in such a rush that he might have been unpacking anyone's old clothes; he set down his case and unbuttoned his greatcoat, although he had been the one to mention the cold. Not turning round, preoccupied with his great-coat, he muttered, 'I've come to you on a certain matter; they should have let you know, put you in the picture, so to speak. So I've come about this business, I'm going to get to the bottom of it . . . '

Still half-asleep, Khabarov took the warrant officer to be spotless, glowing, as though of very high rank, and he stood bewitched by the man's listless, whining voice. Then suddenly, realising, he shrieked, 'You've come from the comrade general!' Slamming the door and grabbing his boots, he lunged for his trousers and tunic. 'I can't believe it!' The captain's head was spinning and in his excitement he was shaking all the bits of uniform he had picked up. Then, looking out of the window, he fell back, dazzled. 'What's that? They sent a truck? He promised me, he promised. He said, "I'll send you everything, show me what you can do!"'

Initially completely stunned by what he had heard, Skripitsyn moved – he sat down on the chair and said, 'Well, then. What's he like, this here general?'

'Oh, what a man, what a man! He asked all about it and got right to the heart of it . . . He's far away, but he knows everything, just like he was standing next to you! It's incredible . . . A different sort would eat you alive, entrails and all, but this one takes you at your word, and praises you . . . ' Khabarov was yelping and running about the office, which made it seem more cramped than ever.

However, Skripitsyn had fused with the chair and turned into wood. 'You mean he praised you?' He forced the words out.

The captain stopped short and straightened his tunic. 'So are potatoes like stones? You can't boast about growing them?'

'This is the first I've heard of this guff you're spouting,' said the special investigator, cutting him off. 'Skripitsyn is my name, I'm from the Special Department, perhaps you've heard about it. You all know it, comrade Khabarov, don't play the idiot; quit feeding me these fables about the general.'

The captain's shoulders drooped. He sat down on the unmade bed; this put him face to face with Skripitsyn, who frowned at him sourly. 'If it's the Special Department . . . You mean the general didn't send you?'

'Oh leave off, Khabarov, that's not even funny any more.'

'I can't make head or tail of this. Since when did the Special Department have a sense of humour? If you've come, then what for?'

'I thought you'd gathered your thoughts, so to speak, you'd confessed. I thought we'd quickly get everything sorted out. But I see you're very stubborn. Let's begin, then. You'd best start getting used to it, citizen, if that's how it's going to be.'

Skripitsyn reached for his briefcase, looked into its depths and, plunging his arm in almost to the elbow, stirred around in its bottomless maw before dragging out a cardboard folder, one of those in which 'dossiers' are put together. However, this folder seemed atrophied, apparently from not having enough to do. Under its cardboard cover lay several sheets of dried-out paper, looking like someone's flayed hide. Peeling them off and handing them sternly to the captain, Skripitsyn left the folder completely bare.

'What's this for?'

'Read and you'll find out.'

'Go on, tell me, I'll understand that way, I'm not deaf.'

'What's this? Have you forgotten how to read, too?' Skripitsyn snorted.

'You find everything funny,' said the captain, and listlessly took all the papers just as they were given him.

Khabarov was unused to reading. It was difficult for him to understand things on paper; it was like groping around in the dark. For this reason, even in front of Skripitsyn, he set about reading aloud. Skripitsyn grew annoyed – he thought the captain was putting this on, taking the piss. But the captain was reading sullenly for his own benefit. He had forgotten about the investigator and was reading the denunciations.

He stumbled in places; he would read the words out a second time, and then he would blurt out in surprise: 'Oh, the bastards!' Skripitsyn had to sit motionless, listening to the captain's loud monologue, and seeing with astonishment that the captain was not at all cowed by the words he was reading – he was clearly and unhurriedly enunciating each one in measured tones. When the papers had been read through, Khabarov wordlessly placed them on the table but then, seeing that the investigator didn't understand a thing, went ahead and said his piece. 'This one was written by Sinebriukhov, the camp commandant. I don't know about this one . . . Many soldiers have deserted, they go to Dolinka. Some run for it in the summer, others maybe go in the spring, due to the lack of food.'

Returning to his bunk, Khabarov spoke calmly and distinctly. 'I remember now: that Smershevich, the boss of you specials, was here once. He liked to fling papers about, too. Obnoxious individual.' Khabarov did not know what else to say to the special investigator, but he hesitated to escort him back out, now that he was here.

'Memory not coming back?' enquired Skripitsyn, in the hope that this was precisely the case. 'It's just that Smershevich is no longer with us. Pardon me, he burned up.'

'Turns out he couldn't hack it, so they signed him off . . . ' said Khabarov, unwillingly.

'No, that's not it, he actually burned to death, in a fire! Last winter. Didn't anyone mention it? That there'd been a fire at the regiment? It's like a different world here . . . If you're going to light that stove, better set it on a metal plate. They can give off sparks. Maybe you don't quite realise who I am. If they had told you I was coming, you'd know I'm in charge of the Special Department, in place of Smershevich.'

'A warrant officer . . . ' Khabarov looked him over.

'A senior warrant officer,' Skripitsyn corrected him, and reached for the folder. 'Well, then, now that we've refreshed our memories, let's start drawing up the charge sheet. That's, pardon me, enough reminiscing.'

Khabarov suddenly grew indignant, not knowing how to take this at all. 'What do you mean, "charge sheet"? Sinebriukhov wrote lies. And lots of my soldiers have run off to Dolinka prison camp. At Dolinka the work's a bit easier and the grub's more filling, which is why the most incorrigible men get sent to me, for punishment. But give 'em time, they'll come running back, because life with me has got sweeter. They'll make Dolinka the punishment battalion, and then what? You'll whisk yourself off to Dolinka and wave reports under their commander's nose?'

Skripitsyn responded with ingratiation, which might have been taken for trust. He clapped shut the folder with an emphasis the captain did not miss. 'All right, let's leave the charge sheet for now. Maybe we'll get by without any charge sheets . . . You see, I understand you, comrade Khabarov; you could say, I share your . . . Well, what do you suggest, where do you see the causes of this regrettable situation?'

'I'm telling you: look for the people who are stealing!' cut in Khabarov without thinking.

'Well, who's objecting to that?' Skripitsyn dodged the captain's suggestion. 'My job is to find the guilty. Maybe even the regimental commander is guilty. My job is to establish the truth.'

The captain took heart: 'I'll tell you to your face, everything we have has gone rotten.'

Skripitsyn was on his guard. 'Well, if everything we have . . . If it's gone rotten . . . I understand. I for one believe you. But you just put down in writing what's going on in the regiment. I'll send the document off where it needs to go. There's going to be an inspection, soon. They'll sort out where the truth lies and who's to blame. And in the meantime I'll watch your back, as long as you don't stitch me up.'

'I'll make a statement, I'll put it in writing, but they'll convict an innocent man.' Khabarov hesitated. 'Mind you, they're good folk at the regiment! You wait months for a delivery, but they send out special investigators in trucks for nothing.'

There's no telling exactly what the captain was going through, although he actually felt sorry for this conscripted man. However, Khabarov's office had grown depressing; it had become an interrogation chamber. He was depressed by the greasy bare walls, by the bed that looked more like a bench. And by the desk at which the investigator had sat himself down. The captain was frozen through by a prison-cell chill. Skripitsyn paled. 'Well, if that's how it is, we'll continue the interrogation.'

'You mongrel! You get in everywhere, sniffing about, you make me sick. We harvested the potatoes, and stored them. I won't say anything more.'

'You've got a high opinion of yourself, if you think I'm sniffing around you. I'm standing here in defence of national interests. It's you who needs the statement. Otherwise, you see, I'll be forced to impound all your potatoes. The inquiry's already under way, after all; you can't stop it. I'll take them off to the regiment and hand them over for safekeeping. But the potatoes will spoil while they try and work out where they came from. They'll write them off, feed them to the pigs. Do you understand what will happen to all your hard work if all the rules are followed? But there's always someone who will do you a favour, so it will be better if you and I get along.'

And then something happened which Skripitsyn hadn't been expecting at all: the captain had grown so angry that he lunged towards the desk and with a great sweep of his arm all the denunciations covering it were sent flying. If Skripitsyn hadn't snatched up the charge sheet, then the cardboard folder would have plummeted to the floor, too. 'What the hell are you doing in my office?' roared Khabarov. 'You're up to no good, but I've been living here for years! I've been living for this day; I'm not scared of dying. And somehow you think you can take away my happiness with just a piece of paper? I've spent my whole life in torment over this, and you think you can simply take it away and throw it to the pigs, for pity's sake?' Skripitsyn was mesmerised by how simply and easily the captain swept to the floor documents that, had they been put in other hands, could have destroyed him even more easily.

It might have occurred to him that this was because the captain was privy to something even more powerful than the contents of these documents.

The special investigator sat down and apprehensively set about picking his documents off the floor. 'Look how hard you're trying!' the captain shouted, trembling.

Skripitsyn stashed everything back into his case and said, in a sort of questioning voice, 'So you're refusing to make a statement?'

'You'll not chew me up, you'll choke. This has to happen. There are so many mouths to feed. Give them all potatoes! And you like them, too, I can see that . . . You must, if they're fried in lard! In lard, I'm telling you!' Khabarov emphasised the lard, seeing joyfully that the trembling investigator had thrown his arms around his briefcase and greatcoat and was shrinking back from him towards the door; now he leapt away as though he'd encountered something monstrous.

Calming down, the captain sighed in disappointment, 'I swear, I want to rattle him up, knock some sense into him . . . ' The other man's unexpected flight brought peace to Khabarov – and a kind of sympathy.

'But who's to blame?' he wondered, disappointed.

Hearing a noise from the square, he hurried to look out of the window, thinking that the regimental lorry was pulling away.

In the square, the man from the Special Department was yelling at the soldiers crowded round. One of them noticed that the captain was taking it all in and waved his arms like someone drowning. In a daze, Khabarov ran out onto the square.

The Special-Department agent turned away. Next to him, scowling, his faithful acolyte stood braced, ready to launch himself against all of them. The soldiers, growing braver and surrounding the strangers, began to wail: 'Comrade Captain, he's ordering us to load up the potatoes.'

'Tell 'im to piss off!'

'It's Khabarov who gives the orders round here.'

'Don't raise a panic, lads!' The captain could hardly make himself heard over his men, but the crowd grew quieter. He turned to the Special-Department agent. 'You'd do that? Listen. Leave, while the going's good.'

'I've been ordered by Pobedov to take the potatoes to the regiment.'

'Bullshit! You're sheltering under the regimental commander?'

'Captain Khabarov, do you understand that I am from the Special Department?'

'But do you understand, comrade Skripitsyn, that you're bullshitting? Lads, don't listen to this piece of crap!'

'Do you understand what he's dragging you into?' shouted Skripitsyn, turning to the men. 'There isn't any general . . . It was the regimental commander Pobedov who rang this idiot. An idiot who'll be under arrest by tomorrow!' A shower of mud and stones rained down on the investigator, who made no attempt to protect himself, although he did see one handy soldier aiming vengefully at his head, who was filled with silent joy when his rock struck the peaked cap from the warrant officer's head.

'Stop pissing about! Whoever's throwing stones, leave off, bloody hell! That's just what he's waiting for.' The captain was agitated; he interposed himself in front of Skripitsyn, to cover him.

'We should go, it's about to kick off . . . ' Sanka whispered, but his boss shrugged him off angrily.

'You animals! Animals!' yelled Skripitsyn, lurching forward, and the soldiers rushed to get out of his way.

'Khabarov is our commander. If he gives the order, then we'll start loading!' shouted the soldiers to the Special-Department agent as they scattered throughout the yard, leaving Khabarov and Skripitsyn alone in the middle of a cold, slushy ring.

They stood facing each other, so dissimilar, so alien, that they would never see eye to eye. 'Kolodin,' snapped the investigator, 'is the order clear to you? Carry on, don't be afraid.' Kolodin stepped firmly off towards the shack. The soldiers waited in perplexity, not approaching. When he dragged the first sack out from the shack, Khabarov sagged to the ground and yelled violently, 'Lads, those are ours!' However, the men were silent and kept their distance, waiting for something, already a little afraid of the Special-Department agent.

The captain stumbled and collapsed; he'd run out of energy. He got to his knees and stared mindlessly at Skripitsyn, moaning: 'I'll place you under arrest myself, I'll . . . I'll shoot you!' With unsteady hands he unholstered his pistol and brandished it at the men, shaking and rocking. But Skripitsyn stood his ground – he didn't believe for a second that Khabarov had enough courage to shoot. And then Sanka leapt awkwardly at the captain, pulling the trigger with all the strength he could muster. A snap shot rang out, the heavens rang, and their dirty blue hue was shaken. Safe and sound, but limp from delayed shock, Sanka yelled, 'I've got him, he's for it now!' Following Skripitsyn's orders, the captain was tied up and locked in the armoury, which had an iron roof, no windows and a grille instead of a door. He was still hurling himself about and yelling, 'Seize him, lads! Get him, my boys!' Once they had dragged Khabarov into the armoury, the Special-Department agent turned his gaze upon the captain's pistol, now lying unclaimed on the ground. He picked it up and stashed it in his briefcase.

The cleverer soldiers stole away from the square so as not to be set to work. But the ones whose curiosity kept them rooted there were grabbed by Skripitsyn and put under Sanka's command to drag the potatoes into the lorry. Dejected, they flung the sacks into the lorry with something approaching fury, which meant the loading proceeded without hindrance; quite swiftly, in fact.

As it turned out, the *zeks* had been watching what was unfolding in the barracks square for some time, sitting in crowded ranks on the roofs of their own barracks. They suddenly took it on themselves to begin an incessant whistling in solidarity with the heavily laden soldiers.

There, on the prison-camp barrack roofs, distur-
bances had started that were quickly turning dangerous.
They set one of the roofs alight and flames soon took
hold. Shots began rattling out from the sentry towers.
The *zeks* reluctantly withdrew back into the zone. Only
the camp juveniles remained on the barrack roofs, like
parched saplings. They knew no fear because they hated
everything around them, as though born to it. Knowing
that the machine-gunners wouldn't dare shoot at them,
the young lads started showing off, flinging down slates at
the soldiers heading away from the barracks. Only when
Kolodin was already fastening down the cover on the lorry
did the prison warders clamber up onto the roofs. They
laid into the teenagers with long steel rods – reinforcing
bars – chasing and grabbing them. They swung the last
few by their hands and feet and tossed them off the roof.

The square emptied of people. The sole warrant
officer in the company ran in from guard duty. Skripitsyn
had sent for him. The enforcement agent handed over
command of the company to him, ordering that Captain
Khabarov be neither untied nor released. He also promised
an escort for the arrested party to arrive the very next day.
The warrant officer – who had the aspect of a legendary
warrior – had only one response to all the arrangements
being made by the investigator: silence – although his
expression suggested disagreement. He nodded and shook
his head, but never once opened his mouth for fear of
himself being arrested, should the investigator smell the
fumes on his breath. His mournful, drink-ravaged face

eventually sickened Skripitsyn so much that he stopped mid-word and waved his hand, then made his solitary way to the lorry.

As soon as the lorry started up and moved off, its engine rumbling, a great howl went up, as if all the guard dogs in Karabas had woken up; as if even the steppe itself had found a voice and suddenly taken up an indistinct, rumbling howl.

The lorry drove off. Far from the camp settlement, its faint headlights formed the sole illumination in the whole darkening steppe.

Towards December, the heavens simply collapse; from them fall great torrents of numbingly cold rain, often mixed with snow. The winds drive cold air about, honing it so its gusts cut through everything living, even the steppe grasses. The earth chills. The steppe track is squelched into a filthy quagmire, which gets smeared across junctions and sharp turns.

Huddled into his greatcoat, Skripitsyn kept opening and closing his eyes; Sanka could not make out if his boss was dozing or fretting. They were rolling along a level strip of land that was swathed in mud. Suddenly a rut narrowed. The lorry shook jarringly. Skripitsyn gave a moan. Sanka instantly slowed down. 'Put your foot on it!' ordered his boss at once.

'I can't just here. The wheels will spin in the mud and we'll get bogged down.'

'Faster, drive faster!' said Skripitsyn with a grimace, not understanding what had been said.

'Punish me if you like, but I have to answer for you.'

'Oh, shut your mouth!' exclaimed Skripitsyn. 'Listen here. Turn off the road, head straight onto the steppe. Drive!' Skripitsyn was gasping for breath; his dry eyes were shining like a dog's. He floundered about in the cramped noisy cab as though he meant to stand upright in it. The lorry had driven off onto the steppe and was forging along, God knows where to. It rattled over the bumps and shook from side to side. And then, with a grinding noise, they were flung from their seats, while the lorry, which had nearly turned over, dug deep into the earth and stalled. Sanka came to with the sour taste of blood in his mouth and a nagging pain around his ribs. He bellowed and spat something onto the floor. Skripitsyn was gazing worriedly at his bloodied acolyte.

'My chest hurts,' the other man complained, and the agent turned away from him. 'Are you all right?' mumbled Kolodin, but heard nothing in reply. He quietly spat out the rest of the blood, wiped himself up and tried to start the engine with a shaking hand. The lorry spluttered and slipped a little.

'Are we stuck fast, then?' asked Skripitsyn, all of a sudden.

'We'll get ourselves out, we'll get going again . . . '

'We won't drive anywhere, get out,' Skripitsyn said, with determination. 'You throw the potatoes out of the back, we'll sink them in this puddle.'

'How come? You said yourself, orders came from Pobedov to take them to the regiment.'

'I'm my own Pobedov . . . What do you know about my life, you idiot? It's me, I command everyone.'

'First you say take the potatoes, that was the order. Then you say there is no order, chuck them away. But maybe I'm also a person. What do we need to do that for?' And then Skripitsyn lost his patience and blurted out: 'The reason you're a person is that I saved you. Or have you forgotten? I saved you; I didn't shrink away from you in disgust. When I say jump, you jump, just as I said!' Sanka dumbly submitted to this command and climbed out, and into the back of the lorry.

Skripitsyn climbed out after him and walked off a little, then stood motionless on the empty expanse of steppe. He stood there bare-headed, his wits seemingly addled by the steppe winds. He was looking askance at the mud into which the potatoes were being poured, and to his eyes they came alive: they snored gently in the sacks as the tireless Sanka lifted them; as he threw them overboard, they shrieked, raining down; and they droned on in the mud.

Eventually, they formed a mountain. 'There, that's it, now they've spoiled . . . ' mumbled Skripitsyn under his breath.

When it was all over, the lorry started up and moved off, but rather than plunging still more angrily ahead, it crawled heavily backwards onto the potato pile, flattening it down and then grinding it with its wheels, until nothing was left there but a raw paste.

4

A MATTER OF STATE

His eyes bleary with fatigue, Kolodin missed the moment when, having been dragged along the steppe through the ruins of mining villages and through little towns that stood empty along its edges, the highway seeped finally into twilit Karaganda like a sluggish, laden-down river. He'd confused the fires blinding him with the fainter fires in Karaganda. The lorry sped along dingy, flat, leaden squares and swerved its way between blocks of flats, lifeless in the night-time that squeezed down on them; it scared the sleeping side streets and sneaked through deserted junctions.

Although the Karaganda regiment was based within the city boundaries, it was surrounded by open spaces and ground that had been dug into by abandoned foundations and trenches. Here, in the middle of nowhere, it was further hidden by a concrete wall that looked like a long, wide road, although the road only led along its own closed circle.

This wall could only be traversed by way of the long road that encircled it, ending in a kind of funnel, where a gate suddenly appeared: an abyss of gaping black steel. In it, though, there was a little door, as if to a house; not for vehicles, this, but for people. Hanging above the gateposts were lamps, burning inside steel muzzles. The place was empty, and hollow. The same lamps shone melting paths down into the mire at the gates, where the mud had been churned up during the day.

They'd stopped expecting anyone to arrive at the checkpoint a good while earlier – they were relaxing for the evening, playing cards. Skripitsyn was asleep. Sanka went to the gatehouse himself. There he waited, while their arrival at the regiment was recorded in the logbook. As happens towards nightfall, a certain cosiness had set in at the gatehouse. The duty officer who had been dragged away from the card game by this whole procedure – just by looking at him you could tell he was a kind man – stamped and signed the record, giving a cheery wink to Sanka. 'So where's that secret boss of yours? Worn out, is he? Taking a nap?' As soon as Kolodin appeared on the threshold, the soldiers on sentry duty in the guardroom went silent and stared at him; they stared reproachfully at the acolyte of the Special-Department head until he left, as though he had no right even to be in the same room as them.

The officer sat briskly back down to his cards, exclaiming, 'Oh, what I'd give for more hearts!'

One of the sentries grimaced unhappily. 'Them buggers get to ride in lorries. All right for some . . . '

'Everyone knows that Skripitsyn is a crawler,' the officer could not restrain himself. 'He'd kiss a toilet seat, if he thought it would get him promoted. There's never enough butter for that one, he always wants it spread thicker!' Meanwhile, outside the grilles on the gatehouse windows, the cast-iron gates were clattering as they slowly parted, opening for the waiting lorry.

Nothing was stirring on the regimental parade square when it came up under a searchlight beam arcing down from an iron mast erected above the roofs.

There were boxy constructions that could only be told apart by their smell, which hit you from some distance off – one, from the bathhouse, smelt as though they were drying out damp cats; another, rotten, was from the cookhouse – these were arrayed along the edges of the square like sentry boxes. Above the huge regimental square there hung a faint black cloud, in which the searchlight beam played like a vein of sparks of mysterious origin. The air itself had turned into a government-issue machine, fit for breathing in and out.

At this time of night the regiment was deathly quiet. Once the soldiers had eaten, they were led in a column to the crappers, where by company and platoon the final evacuation of the day – there were supposed to be three, in all – took place. After this, the soldiers were led into the barracks, and if nobody did anything out of line, lights-out was soon called. The barracks stank of puttees, even though they used to beat up men who hadn't washed theirs for months. It also stank everywhere of bleach, like someone else's piss. There was a standing order in the regiment, when it came to disinfection: pails full of bleach stood everywhere. To get into the cookhouse you had to dip your hands in the pail; only then would they let you eat. After crapping you were also supposed to wet your hands in the pail. The bleach ate away at your hands so that, with time, they began to look more like dead wood, and even started to rot.

Kolodin drove out onto the square and stopped by the headquarters, a powerful stone building surrounded by bushes. Skripitsyn came round slowly and shook himself out of the lorry. Limping a little, he dragged himself off to the HQ, almost dead on his feet, but near the entrance he bumped into one of the junior staff officers, who seized tight hold of him, and apparently did not intend to let go. 'You what? Do you know already? You running off? Are you heading for a fall, Skripitsyn?'

'I don't know what you're talking about!' spluttered the investigator, pushing the other man away in irritation.

'Oh, he doesn't know! Bless him! Pobedov has roused the whole regiment – "Where's Skripitsyn? Bring me Skripitsyn . . . " He had a right go at me, about my tie being wrinkled. But I said to him my tie had been ironed. What are you up to, then? You've shat all over the old man's wellbeing, and you're off into the bushes?' They were pushing and shoving in the dark, scarcely able to see, finally tumbling into the brightly lit entrance with their arms wrapped round each other. 'Good grief, Skripitsyn,' came the staff officer's shrill cry. 'Have you been digging graves?' And the man backed away in fear, then set off at a run. Unexpectedly left in peace, Skripitsyn doubled over as though hit in the stomach and groaned, 'Damn you all, you miserable, cowardly freaks!' Lights were on in all the HQ windows. One window probably shone bright every night – the office window of Fyodor Fyodorovich Pobedov, the regimental commander – even when the rest of HQ was fading into twilight. The old colonel made himself stay at work into the small hours, so those around him would never imagine that he was napping, or absent.

Pinched and diminished, Skripitsyn flitted through the door to HQ like a mouse through a drain hole. Such agility was not necessary to get into HQ, but the agent had been put through the wringer by all that had happened, so was feeling rather like a mouse. He slipped up the empty staircase to the first floor, the colonel's, and calmed down. Then he ran along the corridor, keeping close to the walls, but when he eventually pressed himself up against that massive door behind which raised voices had already been audible for a while, one of the other office doors suddenly flew open and a fat clerk with thin lines instead of lips and eyebrows stepped out. Skripitsyn instantly stood up straight and turned to her, thinking up the fibs he would need on the fly. The clerk, though, gave a great 'Ugh!', making her breasts swell out like clouds, as if no mere mouse but a great rat had appeared before her. She scurried back into the office in disgust. This being the second occasion that someone had shied away from him as if he were a leper, Skripitsyn lost all self-control.

He forgot his fear and burst into the anteroom to learn without further ado what had happened to the colonel while he, Skripitsyn, had been away from the regiment.

In the anteroom, which had that sour smell that usually develops in empty rooms, were two of the less insignificant men in the regiment, standing in very straightforward positions: one opposite the other, arms by their sides. These two were Senior Lieutenant Sokolskii, eternal duty officer in the HQ, and Lieutenant Colonel Petr Valerianovich Degtiar, the adjutant.

The lieutenant colonel looked like a nail: straight, durable, somehow even ferrous. This was a man ashamed of his bald spot; he concealed it under his peaked cap, which he would only remove at Party meetings. Sometimes they would hammer him deep into some matter and could only extract him again with difficulty. Sometimes he got bent in the line of duty, but then they could always knock him straight and try hammering him in again.

When the figure of Skripitsyn appeared on the threshold, standing skewed and, as ever, holding tight to his pitiful, freakish briefcase, the staff officers stopped in their tracks; you might have thought they'd been having a friendly chat about him. Skripitsyn definitely imagined collusion in their silence, and he burst out, 'I want to speak to the colonel. I know he's expecting me!'

At this, Degtiar said, 'Anatolii, you're covered in blood,' and looked concerned.

'The anteroom is full of mud,' Sokolskii added, and barred the scurrying warrant officer's intended route.

'There is a lot of mud,' echoed Degtiar. 'Anatolii, you can't go in to the colonel like that, it's not right.'

'Let me through,' pleaded Skripitsyn, cowed.

'I won't let you through, and I won't even report that you're here,' insisted the senior lieutenant.

'No! You'll let me through!' shouted the investigator convulsively.

They would probably have come to blows if the door had not suddenly been flung open and Fyodor Fyodorovich Pobedov himself had not appeared with words that he had prepared in advance: 'What on earth is going on here? This is the regimental commander's office, not some street market!' Lost to all in his office, hiding behind its pleasant, peaceful walls like a frog in the muck of a swamp, the colonel had a trick of leaping out and catching people so suddenly that the belief spread he was omnipresent. Thin, but with a belly like someone had stuffed a pillow up his tunic, robbed of height, with bulging eyes that seemed ever surprised, and as hard as twice-baked bread, overall Fyodor Fyodorovich Pobedov was a man who had been brought into being not through love, but fear. When calm, he was all wrinkled and faded, making himself quiet and even submissive, while turning noticeably stupider. Mind you, once provoked, he instantly took on such strength that he shook with its gravity, and was remarkable for his blind rages.

'Fyodor Fyodorovich, they won't let me through!' Put on the spot, Skripitsyn lost his nerve. The colonel took offence. Looking apprehensively into the corners and saying nothing, he hustled the warrant officer quickly into his office and shut himself in behind.

In his office, the colonel pounced on Skripitsyn and started bawling at him, giving free rein to his torments: 'Have you no shame, you little shit? You're a filthy tramp and you smear shit on everything around you!'

'Fyodor Fyodorovich, I'm sorry. I'll put it all right, there won't be a stain left on you . . . '

'He'll put it right! The mirror, man, just look in the mirror – do you understand quite what sort of shit you look like in my office?'

Turning painfully to the mirror, Skripitsyn saw his full reflection smeared across the bulky silver plate: his greatcoat was all covered in brown steppe mud; the splashes had reached right up to his chest, where they hung like medals. His face looked as though people in boots had been walking across it: it was bloodied, and plastered with more of the same mud. He shuddered and peeled himself away from the mirror, turning back to the colonel. Vacantly, yet triumphantly, he said, 'I was shot at.'

Hearing this, Pobedov shrank deep within his tunic. Cheered by the effect this had had on the old man, Skripitsyn puffed out his chest and hastened to report, 'I was at Karabas, at Sixth Company, Captain Khabarov's . . . ' And, after a pause for breath, he blurted out: 'Khabarov met me with a bullet.'

'That can't be right!' buzzed the colonel. 'Pack that in. I called the Sixth yesterday, as we agreed, and set things to rights. I explained everything to this captain, and he grasped it. He's a mild enough bloke. I went through it all with him and tore a strip off him like you asked, oh, and then some!'

'How come, Fyodor Fyodorovich,' said Skripitsyn, in exasperation, 'you tore a strip off him and yet, when I got there, they treated me like a nobody?' Pobedov barked: 'Don't overdo it; you are a nobody, aren't you? There's only one regimental commander here.' The agent subsided and started mumbling. 'But this captain called you a general. Said some general rang him. Does this mean you're a general, Fyodor Fyodorovich? Have you been promoted?'

The colonel stepped back and sat down, snatching at a chair that was facing the other way. It had become difficult for him to stand. In his upset, he started speaking earnestly, trying to forestall Skripitsyn; that is, trying to come down still harder on him: 'I always remember what I say; your regimental commander isn't a clown. Don't confuse me. What do you mean, a general? What are you snivelling on about, what are you staring for? What did you report to me, you little shit? Wasn't it that a year's supply of potatoes had gone missing at the Sixth? But if the potatoes are in fact all there, then what's to punish? Or is everyone here telling me lies? Argh! Seems I already made the right decision. I bollocked the captain for acting without orders. I approved the fact that the potatoes were all there. Let 'em carry on, at least they can all eat! And you, you fucker, again you've messed it all up. Yet again. Listen, you portable monstrosity, I'm tired. You drive me mad. I'll send you to court myself.'

'Does that mean you've already sorted everything out yourself, Fyodor Fyodorovich?' said Skripitsyn, feigning surprise.

Pobedov really did not want to answer; it was only anger that made him yell: 'Oh, leave it alone, man! What are you hassling me for? What I want to do, I'll do, seeing as I'm regimental commander.'

'I only acted for the best, Fyodor Fyodorovich . . . ' Skripitsyn was trying to cover his back. 'I thought: "What will they say about us?" There's an inspection on the way.'

Hearing of the inspection, the colonel began fidgeting at the desk. 'But what about the general? What was this crap your captain was spouting about a general? After all, there's a general coming to us for the inspection.'

'That's what I'm telling you, Fyodor Fyodorovich, you haven't thought about the kind of creature this captain is . . . He didn't seek your permission over the potatoes, so of course you couldn't have given it. You'd have had to go first to the divisional commander to get permission, and then maybe even higher, to Central Command. So the matter has nothing to do with potatoes, really, but with the fact that a man like that, with nothing to lose, like this Khabarov, has dared to go against the rules. Turns out this is a political problem. Such people are more dangerous than any infectious illness. He got this vegetable patch of his going. I might add: he fired the first shot! Be sure of one thing: you've got company commanders in the regiment who fire point-blank at the head of the Special Department . . . ' The colonel took fright and called the agitated agent closer to him. 'Well, now, don't get worked up. Sit down.' Then he pondered, and muttered confidentially, 'Now, these potatoes . . . What shall we do with them now, eh? Maybe we should hand them to the security organs? But what about this captain?'

'I've got him under arrest for now, back there in Karabas.' Skripitsyn did not flinch. 'The security organs, they're not exactly a loving mother. You were right when you said we got into a right mess with these potatoes. It would be better if not a soul knew about them; if they all disappeared, or rotted away completely.'

'Everything must be done as the law demands . . . '

'That's right, Fyodor Fyodorovich, but you don't need to think about that. Take it as read that I'll take all responsibility myself. I've already seen to it that there are none left.'

'You've planted them back in, or something? Anatolii, look, stop driving me up the wall.'

'Now don't you worry, Fyodor Fyodorovich, I am indebted to you. I did everything necessary.'

'But what about the captain, what should we do with this Khabarov?'

'Leave Khabarov to me. I'll put a full stop in his dossier, in a way that won't cause a fuss.'

'Ah, this weighs me down . . . It's a strange old dish to be cooking up just before an inspection, of all things.'

'But Fyodor Fyodorovich, who said we have to scoff it all down now? Cases, they take a long time to prepare . . .

We'll have the trial after the inspection has happened, so that the regiment looks all fluffy.'

'All right, make your own decision on this; only, I know nothing about it.'

Looking at Fyodor Fyodorovich, it was clear that he gained in strength as he arrived on duty, appearing a dashing chap, with firm, freshly shaved cheeks and in a tunic that fitted him well – perhaps he had had it specially tailored. By the end of the day, though, Pobedov already looked wrung out, his cheeks sagged and the rosiness that appeared shortly after shaving turned into blueish stains through which grey stubble poked like a pin-cushion. Skripitsyn could not hold back and asked the old colonel suddenly, 'So why were you looking for me, Fyodor Fyodorovich? I was imagining all kinds of things on the way here.' And the colonel, who had been intent on dismissing this bearer of bad news, felt his heart ache, as though a worm had crawled into it. Pobedov was remembering why he had sought Skripitsyn out, although he now feared to say, so he flushed and yelled cantanker-ously in reply, 'When the regimental commander calls, you are duty bound to present yourself. Present yourself and make your report! You're a little shit, but the com-mander's been looking for you all day, because you are duty bound to present yourself and report.'

On removing himself from the colonel's office, Skrip-itsyn inhaled deeply, filling his whole chest, like after a good steaming in the bathhouse. His mood was excellent. 'So, you arse, is your arse not hurting yet?' he enquired, condescendingly, even mockingly, of Sokolskii. The latter was by now sitting in the anteroom that wasn't so much empty as seemingly laid waste by someone, and he had taken hold of some of the papers he found hateful; even their colour was grey. 'Silence!' the lieutenant shot out, suppressing the envious lump that caught eternally in his throat. 'I apologise, comrade General,' Skripitsyn bowed low, with an obsequious expression. 'It's my fault. If you would, apply your belt to my backside.' Then he smirked and straightened up. 'Listen, comrade . . . general; say another word out of line, and I'll break your neck.' For the pleasure of it, he risked a kick at the heavy anteroom door with his boot, and it flung open with a bang. And he walked out holding himself so tall and straight, perhaps he thought himself some kind of general.

Barely in control after what had happened, Sokolskii burst into the colonel's office, where he had a nervous crisis: 'Again Skripitsyn gets away scot-free. I refuse to understand it! He comes in here, filthier than a pig, but you . . . Again you don't pay any attention. What's he doing, strolling round headquarters, the swine? Where's the honour due us officers?'

'Shut the door, man, shut the door . . . ' said Pobedov in irritation – doorways had been bursting open in his line of sight, which meant his gaze fell as if into a tomb, ending at the distant, mute wall in the corridor of HQ, some twenty paces away.

'No. I won't shut it, and I won't leave,' said Sokolskii, boldly. 'First, you answer me: what gives him the right to insult officers and to tip up in your anteroom as though he's at home in his own hovel?'

'Simmer down, brother, what have you got so upset for? He does a difficult job . . . And shut the door, do you need telling twice?'

'Fyodor Fyodorovich, how can you not see that Skripitsyn is consciously doing you harm? That he's weaving a web around you? And how he looks, the way he looks at you? Have you noticed? Insolent, disrespectful . . . '

'Oof, you're talking out of turn yourself, there. Aren't you at least soaking the drink up with anything? Eat something with it, brother, or else you'll spew up from fright right here, if you see a ghost.'

'Fyodor Fyodorovich!' shrieked the lieutenant. 'I understand, you think it's funny . . . But just you keep in mind: wherever Skripitsyn has been, a fire soon follows. Everyone of higher rank than him – everyone – he hates. The criminal! But do you know how he got that nickname – Lard? It was back when he was still a simple soldier. One day he actually stole some lard from the cookhouse!'

'Well, same here, I nearly ended up before the court. Ah, we all go before the court.' Pobedov smiled wryly. 'And you aren't so simple, either, I've seen. You wait, your turn will come. Don't answer back. I'm in command here. I know better than you. Smershevich, you know, was an old wolf, and he only gave Skripitsyn exemplary appraisals, so you put your fire out. Skripitsyn will be here as long as I need him. And so will you . . . Shut the door, I said, you turd, you'll let all the warmth out! And you will, you know, do your duty . . . ' Confused and tormented, the old colonel bashed the desk in his rage, blurting out: 'If it comes to it, I made you all who you are now, and I'll take you all apart. Limb by limb, if need be.'

Just as Pobedov was striking his desk, staring around with his bulging eyes, his gaze seemed to collide with a slumped figure, twisted around a briefcase, which had suddenly appeared to grow out of the dim HQ corridor as though it were some kind of awful phantom . . . 'Get out!' roared the colonel. However, the phantom had already dematerialised, as though it had never been there at all. Calming down, he turned to Sokolskii, 'Gah, I'm seeing things . . . Anyone would go mad with you lot around. I'm sorry, son. Go brew me a nice hot cup of tea . . . ' Sokolskii instantly skipped out of the room to make some tea for Fyodor Fyodorovich.

Incidentally, the old colonel hadn't been hallucinating at all when he thought he saw Skripitsyn. On leaving the anteroom, the investigator hadn't quit HQ but had gone for a wander instead. He'd walked along the corridor into a dead end, as if planning to take a good run up from that direction. However, as he approached the wall, he had happened to find himself before an inconspicuous door tucked right away in the HQ building. It had a veneered nameplate, which read: 'PV Degtiar'. He went and knocked on this door. The adjutant was just having a bite to eat when this furtive knock came. He had deployed himself at his government-issue desk with his cap covering his bald spot; in one hand he held a biscuit that he'd dipped in some condensed milk, while in his other he had a simple faceted tumbler of steaming liquid. Degtiar's office was more modest than the colonel's: there was no anteroom, no walnut cupboards or elongated desks, no mirror. It did, though, contain a strict tidiness: it was clear that this equipment served just as punctiliously as its owner. When the knock came, Degtiar became embarrassed and hid his biscuit in his desk. 'Petr Valerianovich, can I come in?' A head came round the door. 'I'm sorry, I didn't know you were eating. Enjoy your food, I'll look in later.' The adjutant just managed to recognise the investigator before he vanished again, leaving Petr Valerianovich in solitary silence. Understanding nothing, Degtiar breathed out heavily, feeling a peculiar sense of guilt, for no particular reason.

Worn out, Skripitsyn decided to spend the night in the Special Department, so as not to have to slog all the way to his quarters at the other end of Karaganda. After their wooden building had burnt down, the Special Department had occupied an extension stuck on the backside of the HQ building. It had been so poorly rendered that the plaster had peeled off the sides, so that beams stuck out of its three walls like skinny ribs. There were no lights in the windows and the door was locked. Sanka had yet to make his way back from the garage where he'd had to park the lorry. Sanka actually lived in the Special Department, by Skripitsyn's permission, although just now he had completely forgotten this fact. Skripitsyn dealt with the lock using his personal key, and passed like the wind through the department.

There were three little rooms in total, if you didn't count the cold changing room with its coat stand and basin; they were like train compartments, leading to the office at the end, where the boss worked. They were filled with fireproof cabinets, containing secret souls in paper form. In one of these rooms, behind the cabinets, was Kolodin's nook, where his bed was. Here, Skripitsyn undressed, tossing his shroud-like greatcoat to the floor, followed by his tunic and shirt, leaving himself bare to the waist. His flabby white belly and chest wobbling freely, he stepped into the cold changing room to wash, but when he set the tap running, the duty telephone began chirruping in the department.

Despite his ignoring it, the ringing did not stop.

Skripitsyn shrank into himself: how did anyone know he was still there? Only one man could have known, and only one man could be asking for him. Dragging himself into his shaken-up office, the Special-Department agent found he was not mistaken. Pobedov's choked-up voice squeezed down the receiver: 'Anatolii, he rang me!'

'Who did, Fyodor Fyodorovich?'

'Oh, your Khabarov, that's who!'

'What did he say to you?'

'I didn't speak to him, the piece of shit. I ordered them not to put him through, to break the connection immediately . . . So, what happened then, did you not arrest him? How's this happened, how come he's still at liberty?' Skripitsyn remained silent, and the colonel grew tense: 'Anatolii, are you there? Hello, hello . . . Anatolii, I'm telling you, tomorrow he must be behind bars!' Skripitsyn tried to buy time, asking: 'And the order for his arrest?'

'You go there and nip it in the bud, and I'll take care of the paperwork.'

'Very well, Fyodor Fyodorovich. I'll come to you in the morning and we'll discuss it.'

'There's nothing to discuss. In the morning, you go to Sixth. You've created this mess, so now you can make sure it's all tidied up for me. You're a bunch of shits and scumbags, you should all be buried in a ditch somewhere!'

Skripitsyn tossed aside the beeping receiver, and then gave a dry, rasping laugh, like the breath of a guard dog on the chase. Catching his breath, and picking up the abandoned telephone, he called the regimental switchboard: 'This is Skripitsyn speaking. Did the colonel get a call from Sixth Company? Who made the call? Then put me through right now . . . I'm telling you, put me through. Those orders do not apply to the Special Department. Give me Karabas.' A voice was heard, finally getting through, and he immediately lashed out at it, ramping up the pressure: 'Is that the Sixth? Are you so drunk you can't talk sense? Where's Khabarov? What did you say? You piss-artist, say that again to me and . . . Listen, and remember! You let Khabarov go! Let him go! This is me talking to you . . . Yes, I'm a general! Here are my orders. Don't let him have command. As of now, he is considered relieved of his post. Don't let him near the guards. Do you hear? Don't let him make any calls, we've enough idiots as it is without him. You tell him just that: "idiots".'

Ringing off, Skripitsyn immediately dialled the switchboard again. 'This is Skripitsyn. I've spoken to them . . . If the colonel himself calls the Sixth, let me know . . . You what? Do you want to end up in the Special Department? And if they call from Sixth, put them through to us. We'll figure out what they're after over there.' While Skripitsyn was managing these calls with aplomb, Sanka appeared in the Special Department's annexe. He had had no thought of encountering his boss, but when he heard his voice he realised that Skripitsyn had decided to spend the night there. This had happened before, although learning from last year's fire, Skripitsyn was reluctant to stay in the department at night; and if he did stay, Sanka gave up his bunk behind the fireproof cabinets and went to sleep in the garage. This was why, shifting from one foot to the other, Kolodin waited for a similar order.

Catching sight of Sanka, seared by his gaze, Skripitsyn grew angry. 'What are you up to, why are you lurking behind me?'

'Right, I'll be off to the garage,' said Sanka, stepping back, but Skripitsyn collected himself and changed his mind. 'Hang on a sec. You can sleep later. First, wash down the lorry.'

'Yes sir, I have washed it down already.' Kolodin turned his dark, leathery face away and stepped towards the door, but Skripitsyn still couldn't let him leave the department. 'Wait up, Kolodin, listen to me a minute . . . Those potatoes were dangerous. The order came to destroy them. And all I know is that it was a matter of state. The only ones told were me and the regimental commander, and you, of course. But from now on, you just forget all about it.'

Once he'd said what had come feverishly to mind, Skripitsyn sighed to himself, as he saw how blindly Sanka believed him, how he whined with all their accumulated anguish: 'I knew it, I knew . . . I'm behind you every step of the way, no matter where . . . I'd even kill for you . . . '

'Hey, now, stop that, what are you thinking?' Skripitsyn turned numb. 'Listen, you stay in the department, in the morning clean my coat, and don't take a single step outside.'

'But where will you go, if I stay?' protested Sanka, loyally.

'I'll go to the infirmary, they'll give me a space there. Now you get a good night's sleep.'

Appearing in the sickbay, Skripitsyn woke up the duty orderly and, not bothering with long explanations, demanded a bed for the night in the officers' ward. At the same moment, he wrote off Sanka Kolodin: first, from the roster of the Special Department, sensing that this soldier mustn't be around him much longer. But later, as he took a long time to fall asleep in the empty ward, feeling hungry, and thinking over the best way to get rid of this witness that he no longer required, Skripitsyn caught himself thinking it would be better if this soldier went missing by himself, even if this meant he died. He would have fallen asleep with this thought rippling through his soggy, deadly exhausted brain, had he not suddenly remembered his own boss . . . Smershevich.

Skripitsyn smirked and projected his words clearly into the emptiness: 'Well, just where are you now? You what? You got burned?'

'A fire . . . ' he suddenly thought, with alarm, and recoiling from the idea even in his somnolent state, he came to in an unusually compassionate mood. 'No . . . No.' But all the same, this thought about a fire filled him with a sense of peace. And he remembered the business now, in every detail . . .

It had happened without Skripitsyn's involvement, although it had changed a lot in his life, too. Usually, in the autumn, the city sanitary department would send a lorry to pump out the regimental cesspit, full to the brim by this time of year. The logistics service was responsible for summoning the lorry, but they were having a change of command just then, and they forgot to call for it. In the winter, the cesspit overflowed, which meant areas of the regiment's more intimate places began to be fouled up. It was impossible to scoop out the shit: winter is winter. The only thing that remained was to hack it out, or wait for the spring so it could melt. Of course, if they did hack it out, they would be removing their protection from the cold. Around that time, Fyodor Fyodorovich personally ordered that another, temporary, latrine trench be dug around the back. This was dug out of the frozen ground by seven soldiers who were in the sickbay for treatment. They were brought in so as not to tear healthy people away from their duties, although the healthy ones would never have agreed to build a shithouse. The poorly ones, though, were happy at the prospect of not seeing the inside of the barracks for another week or so. They had already dug a hole as deep as a person when they came upon a lumpy, frozen-over cable; but, not pausing to figure out what was what, they hacked away at it with crowbars as if it was made of rock. The electric shock from the hewn-open cable killed all seven on the spot. When the deaths were investigated, they discovered that HQ had a map of its underground infrastructure, on which the cable was clearly marked by a dotted line. Pobedov hadn't even bothered asking for this map. He'd chosen the place for the shithouse by eye, the old-fashioned way. The investigation, and the fatal incident itself, put a great strain on the colonel. He felt so sorry for the lads who had been killed that it hurt, and he reproached himself, but at the same time he refused to accept he was at fault; it had just been one of those unfortunate events. It was Smershevich who saved the colonel: he made the investigation so convoluted that the seven corpses simply vanished into thin air. Having performed such an important service, Smershevich had expected some particular regard, but the colonel shrank away from him, and secretly began to hate him. Once he even said openly that Smershevich should leave the regiment, to which Smershevich replied that in fact he would remove Pobedov.

And then, out of the blue, a rumour started up that Smershevich was Jewish. It started and spread, trickling in from who knew where. Soon everyone was chanting, 'Yid, Yid . . . ' Surrounded by these whispers, Smershevich started drinking terribly, mortally. It seemed to him that the rumour had been started by Fyodor Fyodorovich himself; that is, by Pobedov. True, the colonel was generous with his use of the word 'Yid'. Threatening everything on God's earth, Smershevich staggered drunk from person to person, crying bitterly, 'Well, who is it who's lying? Do I look anything like a Yid to you?' And if they couldn't convince him otherwise, he would start fighting. The rumour started that same winter. That winter, the colonel began trying to win Skripitsyn over, and many people heard Smershevich threatening his investigator: 'Is this you crawling out of the muck and into the good life? Look, you push ahead, you jump the gun, and I'll have your fat in the fire. You'll remember what you used to be, and the dump I dragged you from.'

Perhaps drunk, perhaps angry at being called 'Yid', Smershevich shortly after burned to death, burning down the department with him. Many of the cabinets, it transpired, were unlocked, which led them to conclude that before his death Smershevich had been rifling through the papers, about half of which had burned up. Anatolii Skripitsyn calculated the losses and led an inquiry into the fire. He was not implicated in the matter because he happened to have been away searching for a deserter at the time; no one even thought of suspecting him.

These were the circumstances through which a person so comical and pitiful to look at was given command of the Special Department by Pobedov. The old man himself had long since served out his time, so they thought he would go peacefully into retirement – but the colonel would not go. By then, he already considered himself an eminent military commander, not knowing – because they weren't reporting it to him – that the soldiers were escaping from the companies and the *zeks* from the camps, where the guards standing sentry were drunk and asleep; that the officers were fighting over the most insignificant appointments and promotions, while in the more distant locations there were unholy levels of drunkenness; that everywhere the very plaster was coming away, while recently a cook had fished a rat out of the cauldron of borscht and sworn mightily, as though the rat were responsible for eating up all the meat in it. 'The rats are stealing it right out of the pan!' he had cried, with righteous anger.

5

RELEASED

The simpleton to whom, in his haste, Skripitsyn had left command of the mutinous company turned out to be none other than Ilya Peregud. The Special-Department agent had driven off from Karabas, leaving this man in the middle of the square. On that ill-starred afternoon, both the square and the camp environs seemed to Peregud to have been turned upside-down. The roof of the barracks hung over the skies as though flourishing leaden wings, while Peregud himself felt badly sick. His nausea was not from what he had been drinking, but because he would have killed for a drink.

In life, Ilya Peregud was sustained by two things, which remained at all times sacred to him, since even in his direst need they couldn't be sold for drink: his Cossack topknot and his Cossack moustache. 'I'm a Cossack from the Don – have you heard of that river?' It was impossible to tear your eyes away when he was saying this! It seemed you might put him in a furnace, but even there his topknot and moustache would not burn away, while Peregud himself would stare out from the blazing coals and the fire would howl and sing 'the riverrrr!' His spirit was neither free nor wild but had sprouted like some perennial weed that would eventually even push its way through bare rock. He hadn't settled down to family life, or a nice little home; he had only the most dissolute pastimes; he had no desire, nor ability, to exert himself, to make any effort at all; he didn't want, as he put it, to turn into a worker ant. And anyway, vodka brought him happiness without exertion, without that hateful ant-like toil. When Ilya Peregud drank to his heart's content, the days were like holidays. Turning to drink from one of the resonant bottles, he felt such delight as perhaps only infants know. Peregud knew a hundred different ways of making vodka – how to distil it from rice, wheat, rotten apples, wood chips, old women's headscarves or sour cabbage soup. He even maintained that, if none of the former was to hand, you could brew it from a mix of soil and water. Just spit in it once, to get the fermentation started! And how marvellously the first shot went down after he woke up. It penetrated right through him, as though he was an unfledged, gaping nestling. In that minute, Peregud became blissfully alive, throwing back his top-knotted head and feeling a warm flutter in his chest. Shot after shot, the nestling grew, unfurling its wings in his chest, which as a result became wide and clear, like the heavens. And then Ilya would take wing!

He took wing like a strong, free bird with bright, singing plumage and little bells in his tail. Rising to heights that took your breath away, from which the very earth seemed no more than a wrinkled walnut, his Cossack spirit sailed or swam in the flowing currents of winds that smelt of tobacco, vodka, the Don river and the smoke of Cossack villages.

Peregud remembered living in such a village with his father. His mother had died early, but their smallholding was rich. He and his father had got along well. But one day his old man set off for Rostov, to trade his berries at the collective farmers' market, and came back on his empty cart, arms wrapped round a younger woman. He settled down with this woman, but didn't stop loving his son. He used to say in front of her, 'I'm leaving the small-holding to Ilya, it's up to him what happens to you after I die; maybe he'll let you stay in the house.' As time went on, the woman grew weary of the old man, and began hankering after his son. She began by fashioning herself into a mother: she'd hug him, kiss him on the forehead and say tender words to him. But suddenly she couldn't hold back and would start trying to suck at his lips.

Ilya was reluctant to complain about her to his father. The old man had grown very attached to her, even if he had brought her back unclad and unshod from the city as though hiring a farmhand. But his stepmother grew angry at Ilya's resistance, and turned nasty. When his father was out, she'd fling off her shirt and walk naked round the house, so that Ilya had to avoid home without his father. However, when his father was home, the lascivious woman would snatch a moment when he'd left the room and lift up her skirt: 'Now then, son, take a look at what I'm hiding for you, my darling . . . ' So Ilya had a lot to bear, driven to exhaustion by hiding the truth about her from his father. One day he finally imparted it all, laying his soul bare. The old man unhesitatingly believed his son. He took a whip to the little slut. He ordered her to spend the night in the cowshed, and for there to be not a trace of her, the toad, come the morning. But he awoke to the sound of a woman's shrieks coming from the cowshed. He ran in and saw that his son seemed to have piled on top of his stepmother, tearing off her shirt and crawling around on her, while she was thrashing about underneath him and yelling. Then the old man forgot about his wrath. He caught his son over the head with a pole. And when Ilya came to, he had neither father nor family home. From the previous evening she had been swearing to the old man as he'd been putting the whip across her that Ilya had spoken up in revenge for her staying faithful to his father, and the son had got nowhere with her.

The old man hoisted his unconscious son onto a horse and turned him in to the police, and when Ilya was convicted of raping his father's wife, the old man lived for another year, then died. The house, the yard, the smallholding with the two horses, pigs, orchard and vegetable patch – all went to that vile woman who had married him to herself, and practically killed him.

The young widow sold it all as a single lot, without haggling, and lightly skipped away from the foreign village she had plundered.

Ilya Peregud drank down misery in the camps until he started vomiting blood, yet he survived due to his natural strength. He did three years and survived, while they made the rest of his sentence easier, having turned him into a *zek*, albeit an unmanageable one, by putting him to unpaid, black-market work.

He was seeing out the rest of his time in Karaganda, meaning his work days were spent on the far reaches of the Kazakh steppe, in a clean little town called Abai, where they had set him to work as a miner. But his soul was not meant for the daily grind and graft. He never even got used to getting up when told to and following orders.

The Kazakh steppes were a kind of God-given homeland for him, like a warm bright sky for a bird. For the Kazakhs who roamed from place to place with the collective farm herds, every guest was dear – they'd feed him up and get him drunk and shed blood for him. They'd give him all the *kumis* he could drink. And, what's more, there's this *araka* stuff, which is even stronger than Russian vodka, oh, yes!

It could be said that Ilya Peregud drank out of his endless fear of sobriety. Either it was mental illness, a portent of the DTs, or out of desperate ignorance or the unceasing viciousness that had built up within him, but Peregud maintained, sometimes with scary intensity, that there was in the world a terrible force seeking to exterminate all Cossacks. In his mind, this force was called 'the hounds'; he wasn't able to express it any more precisely than that. It meant that good order which compels a person to submit.

Once he was released from forced labour, Ilya Peregud stuffed himself with food in the steppes from Karaganda to Zhezkazgan, from Uralsk to Balkhash. Ancient enemies of the Cossacks, the steppe-dwellers were initially somewhat afraid of Peregud, with that moustache and topknot of his, but in time they began to like him. Peregud forgot how to speak Russian, and learned to hunt for steppe game and drink *kumis* without revulsion, but he was a poor worker and his bosses despaired of him. Come winter, the nomads went back to the collective farms, where there was a great mass of Russians and Kazakhs already settled. And their debts had to be paid in full, in cash if you had it or in sweat if you hadn't.

So come winter, Ilya made his way from the steppe to the little mining settlements, but everywhere there were bosses he could not stomach, and low pay, and nowhere to live. Women fell in love with him, but each one wanted only to marry him; only then would they agree to provide food and drink, and to register him as residing in their home. But for Peregud marriage was that same, ant-like, unwanted expenditure of effort; there was no way he could inflict it on himself.

Once Ilya Peregud got lost on the steppe, on his way from one nomad camp to the next in search of the *araka* that gave him life. Halfway there, tormented by his sobriety, he lay down, thinking he'd have a bit of a rest. His dried-out throat itched so much that he wanted to scratch it, if not tear it out. However, the blazing steppe sun bound his arms with tight, fiery strands, so that he slumped on the ground and chewed at what bitter, wasted grass he could get to with his mouth.

And suddenly, from out of the ground reared a wolf. Small, with a rough reddish coat like pig bristles and a bit of beard that irritated the eye like dust. Sharp and wedge-shaped, with a peculiar insolence, this beard gave the wolf's thick, broad-browed muzzle a wrathful appearance. The wolf looked at Peregud with tearful, human eyes, and spoke to him in a roar: 'The time has come at last for you to fear your masters; it's payback time for all the bread you've eaten. You've spent enough time on your spree.' Nothing could have struck Ilya more forcefully than the fact that this wolf, speaking to him in the unpeopled steppe, stank of dried fish: a sober and salty scent, just like blood. Or the stink like you get in a camp barracks. Ilya grasped then that this was the hound himself speaking to him. They each had a pack leader above them, who was drawn from that iron-bristled pack of theirs that feeds on living people.

With the last of his strength, Peregud sprang to his feet and raced away from the wolf. It chased after the Cossack, trotting a short distance behind him, as though dropping back to offer him some hope, which put fresh air in his lungs. But in fact the hound was waiting for this Cossack to run out of breath for good. Ilya ran for a *verst* or so, then crawled on his stomach, clutching at the grass, while the wolf padded along behind him. When, exhausted, Peregud could no longer draw breath, it stood over him and spoke again: 'The time has come at last to be harnessed by your masters. Everyone is already in harness, and we till the soil from their backs. Or have you still not understood that our truth holds sway on this earth? Or do you still believe you are your own master?'

Peregud played dead, but his heart, constricted by fear, beat out from his chest across the whole steppe. The wolf spat out a cough, growing angry at the Cossack's desire to trick him. He said: 'The time has come at last to eat you. It is no good being afraid, save for your flesh and bones. From now on you can look forward to the odd visit from us, and to sacrificing the odd lump of flesh, since you've put some meat on your bones.' The wolf bit off the tiniest morsel, then sprang away from poor, howling Ilya and resoundingly chomped his jaws. The wolf derived no pleasure from what he swallowed; he could not allay his appetite with just one bite. This was his job, his duty as a hound. Looking for a moment with revulsion at the Cossack's vivid torment, he suddenly rose to his hind legs, growing huge, and paced off into the steppe somewhere, to wherever it was he had to go.

Poor Ilya was found by some Kazakhs who had been hunting in the area. They took him to their camp and got him drunk on *kumis*. The steppe-dwellers did not believe his testimony. But not because the wolf had spoken with a human voice. Knowing their lands and the habits of the beasts there from birth, the Kazakhs told the Cossack that there was no way a wolf could appear in their arid steppe. Wolves did not live where there was no open water. So the steppe-dwellers decided that Peregud must have been drunk, since he thought he had seen a wolf. And the chunk of flesh had been gnawed out of him by voles while he was sprawled on the ground. The Kazakhs cared for Ilya diligently, and he spent another month in the camp enjoying their *araka*; he could have wished for nothing better.

But the memory of that reddish wolf muzzle would return to Peregud and his fear would revive when they stopped refilling his glass on the steppe, and when they refused to pour anything for him in the little towns, and again when eventually he could scarcely beg a mug of rancid beer off the labourers. And then again came the stench of dried fish, and it seemed to Peregud that the hounds were seeking him out; they were on his trail.

What's more, in all the years since his spell in the camps, Ilya dreamed one and the same dream: He's been drinking vodka and he's wandering about on his native soil in a posh white shirt. Suddenly he's approached by the guardians of order, who seize him and sling him in the back of a lorry, so tightly enclosed by stinking metal that it seems more like a coffin. His soul is shaken right out of the back of the lorry and he gets thrown into a huge, lifeless house, inside which everything is metallic and rusting, and again there's that smell of dried fish, as though old women are living there. Then he is stripped naked and hosed down with icy water, just as if he's shat himself. The women doing the hosing are so fat they look like blokes. For good measure, while he's still naked and frozen, these massive women give him a good going-over with their boots. Almost dead, he is dragged off and they stretch him out to sleep on a bedframe, tying his hands to it with what is either barbed wire or a guitar string. Come the morning, for further punishment, they shave him, using clippers to make it uglier. They give his things back without the buttons, which for some reason they have torn off, and they laugh at him: 'Look at you, you sorry bastard, you ought to be annulled, you're a disgrace to your motherland.' He takes a look, and his shirt is dirty and torn, and covered in blood.

Although he bore all these tortures, in his dream Peregud could never endure the fact that they shaved off his topknot and moustache with those vicious large-toothed clippers, and he would awake from his suffering in those moments of horror. Tormented by his dreams and by reality, Peregud surrendered: he consciously sold his soul to the hounds, in the supposition that they would not destroy him. This artless deal was struck in Ugolpunkt, in the barracks-like hostel for camp-workers where he was getting drunk with the prison guards; with tears in his eyes he begged his new friends to sort him out a job in the camp administration.

Maybe this had happened in a drunken moment, but once he had been taken on, Peregud served many years.

To begin with, he served as a prison guard – nicknamed 'Sledgehammer' – and then he transferred to the sentry company under Captain Khabarov, as a form of retirement, thinking secretly to himself that the captain, too, was on the run from the hounds; that he, too, although he was hiding it, was one of the last Cossacks.

However, Peregud's unsettling vision came true! Khabarov was arrested, the potatoes taken away, and it seemed to Peregud that the hounds had begun hunting down the Cossacks. Meanwhile, there were no doubts in the company that Peregud would release the captain just as soon as Skripitsyn had got well away. Peregud grew obstinate, saying he was not about to disobey an order. But he still ran for the armoury, where Khabarov had been locked up.

The captain was sprawled in the cage of the weapons room. The metal cabinets in which the weapons were stored ran round the sides in unbroken ranks, which made it seem as though the cage was empty. Khabarov lay silently, like a dead man, but when he heard footsteps approaching, he roused himself and made for Peregud. 'Let me out of here right now!'

Peregud, whom the Special-Department agent had left in charge of the company, simply whined in response: 'There's no way I can do that, Vania, they'll take you before the court tomorrow, just be patient.'

'So you've bought into all that bollocks, too?' exploded Khabarov. 'Well, I spoke to the general yesterday, they're going behind his back!'

'There is no general . . . ' sobbed Ilya. 'You've got to confess, maybe they'll still let you off.'

'You're supposed to be my friend. Who else is going to believe me?' said the captain, deflated. Peregud stepped back out of the cage in silence, hiding his bovine eyes and sobbing. 'The potatoes! Save the potatoes!' yelled Khabarov into the void, and went on yelling until he grew hoarse.

Ilya took the keys to the armoury from the sentry on duty, hid them in his pocket and headed for a quiet corner of the barracks, where he shut himself up in his hovel. Shortly after, he began singing:

'If he hadn't known his own woes, my lads,

he wouldn't have known how to carouse or to quaff.

But if his voice hadn't called out the songs from the Don, my lads,

he wouldn't have known how to sing or to love . . . '

Starving, bereft of the potatoes and the captain's care, the soldiers enacted reprisals on one another, yelling, 'So, did you sell out the captain? Did you sell out our spuds?'

One guilty party was found nevertheless – a soldier by the name of Korneichuk, who simply had not run off anywhere, hadn't hidden, but just moved to one side, smoking tobacco and looking around without interest. Petr Korneichuk believed that his dear mother and father had given him as much strength as there was water flowing in the river. Whoever came at him, he walloped them with his square army belt buckle, so hard that one lad bounced off the floor. The soldiers then lunged for Petr in a mob, which left the square and the entire camp settlement once again devoid of people. They beat him until darkness fell, as though they truly meant to kill him. They hit him until they grew tired, ran away, then came back to hit him some more, but there was no way they could put a mark on his face; waves of attackers kept trying for one really telling blow before once more ebbing away.

They went back for Petr when his share was left over from dinner. They were scared that they had done him in completely, although that rubbery young lad – who it turns out had himself gone looking for revenge with a belt and a buckle on the end of it – maintained that, even after the buckle hit Korneichuk, he had been breathing like a good 'un, and even snuffling, abandoned on the barracks square. In the darkness they didn't immediately make out the fissure. The fissure went right up to the latrine, although the shithouse was empty. The missing man was discovered by accident, when one of the soldiers decided to relieve himself, and from under his arse, freshened by the steppe winds, were heard Korneichuk's groans. They looked through the hole, which was festooned with plumes of newspaper, and were able to make him out, drowning. They threatened, explained and cajoled, to try and get him to come out, but Korneichuk had grown so scared of people that he no longer believed them. Summoned to assist as the commander, Peregud tore a board off the shithouse wall and lashed out with it at the assembled crowd. They all ran away from the enraged Ilya. Left to himself, Peregud had a long and heartfelt conversation with Korneichuk, but the other man would not agree to come out for anything, although he did not talk this through so much as mumble. Angry on the other man's behalf, Peregud knocked down the clapboard shithouse, levelling the latrine. If any member of the rest of humanity had appeared on that steppe just then, their gaze would have taken in an astonishing picture. Boards were strewn over the ground as if after some great catastrophe. Among them, on the bare dark steppe, sat a mysterious warrior who was clutching his top-knotted head and maintaining a muffled monologue, which seemed to be intended for only two people; 'You have to keep living. No matter what they did to you, spite them and live. It's simpler. You can hide in the shit, but then what? You're not going to sit there for ever, are you?' And the ground beneath the warrior whines piteously, at which the warrior bends low and listens. 'Are you still breathing, or what?' And he says, as though entreating the earth itself: 'Come with me; they won't touch you if you're with me. Tell you what, shall I find you a new uniform, one of the really good ones? Listen, come on, let's get one. And we'll get the bathhouse warmed up!' What happened next, no one will ever know. But Peregud somehow did his duty and extracted the man who had been drowning in shit.

•

Karabas plunged into the dark, chilly water of night. On its surface, which appeared shrivelled as though burnt, only the camp searchlights swam. The guard dogs chained to their posts howled mournfully, sensing the complete disorder that reigned in the world of people. That was the kind of night it was when Peregud appeared before the arrested man with a mess tin of peas, a lump of rye bread and a confession. 'Enough! It's beyond my powers to endure any more.' He stuck his hands through the gaps in the locked grille and undid the canvas straps on the captain's numb extremities. Then he pushed through the mess tin and the bread, whispering, 'We'll tell them that you managed to untie yourself.'

The captain was dozing, but when Ilya untied his hands as though he was taking the boots off a drunk, he instantly awoke, catching scent of the peas and bread from within his doze. Khabarov had forgotten that there was such a thing as pease pudding in the world, and that he was supposed to have a ration allotted, and he spent a long time munching up the last traces. 'After all, the general made me a promise . . . ' the captain moaned. Once again he had clean forgotten about his peas; his hands were just wrapped around the mess tin now for warmth. 'There you go again about this general, and he doesn't exist.' Ilya grew sad. 'You be glad that they'll be passing sentence on you. Prison is the most reliable protection from them. They'd shave my head, and there's no vodka, but I'd go myself. What am I talking about, there's no way out for me. But you're a different sort of person. Don't you run away from them, let them pass sentence!'

'You mean you won't let me out?'

'You're a different sort of person, but they'd hound me to death.'

'You want me to sit quiet in prison? Let me call the regiment.'

'Now leave it, Vania . . . '

The captain got up with difficulty and, leaning on the metal front of a gun cabinet, took to kicking it with his boot like he was ringing a bell. 'Ivan, they'll hear you!' Peregud pressed himself up to the grille. 'Damn you, make a noise, then, go to hell!'

And then, in his misery, Ilya performed a heroic deed.

Peregud himself checked the connection and carried the receiver of that terrible device to the captain, as though it contained a bomb ready to explode: 'It's ringing, the son of a bitch. Get ready, Ivan!' The telecommunications apparatus was right up against the grille. At the same moment as Ilya was looking at the captain, shining with a clear light, Khabarov himself was ringing up the regiment, as though returning to a past time: 'Operator, sister mine, it's me, I . . . Captain Khabarov! The Sixth! Where's that general of yours? What do you mean, "no"? Be a dear, look it up, they put me through to him!' Suddenly he shrieked in a frenzy: 'The regimental commander, then. Give me Pobedov, I'll speak to him!' The next moment, he reddened. 'I want to hear it from him, I don't believe you . . . I'm telling you, let him say so!'

But the regiment did not give the captain a chance to get aggressive, and so, hunching over like a mountain, he took to blowing, shouting and banging at the receiver. Eventually, he gave in: 'They cut me off, the bastards . . . '

Ilya shook, and with a great roar he blew the soldiers out of the woodwork: 'Pack up that talking shop, put it back where it belongs!' The proceedings were like a kind of stampede. The device retreated to the office, Peregud carrying it back there in two bounds, like a piece of fluff. It seemed to Ilya that any moment now the barracks would be struck by lightning, or the hounds would attack out of the blue, as a punishment for their sins. He said over and over: 'Oh, we brought it on ourselves! Oh, now we're for it . . . They'll take us first!'

After an eternity, there once more came a ring from the office. From somewhere in that hinterland between life and death, Peregud shambled off in answer to its summons and, afterwards, paced heavily back down the corridor. He held a key-ring on which jangled all the company keys. He silently unlocked the cage and muttered to the captain, who had grown quiet: 'Come on out. It's an order from your general. We've been ordered to let you out, apparently. They said you're an idiot and you're not to ring again. They'll look into your case later, when they get round to it.' Peregud could no longer hold back. 'That's how it'll be. Come out! If you don't want to, you can spend the night there. It's the right place for idiots, behind bars.'

This was how they greeted the morning: Khabarov in his open cage, Peregud in the office, silently and stubbornly waiting for the Black Maria to arrive. But nobody came for Khabarov. The captain left his cage to fetch in a mattress, a pillow and an old greatcoat, and he lay back down. He got up early, went out to freedom after all, and had a wash. They brought his rations into the cage, as he had already refused to come out for his food. The following morning, they brought him nothing: they had forgotten. Towards evening they remembered and brought him some cold pearl-barley gruel. Later in the night, Ilya paid him a visit, out of duty, and ruined everything: 'What are you turning yourself into a scarecrow for? Just be happy you're still alive.'

That night, when no one could see him, the captain paid a visit to the shack where the potatoes had been stored. He went and set up home in there, while awaiting his arrest. When it grew light, Khabarov would go out to the field, which had become so empty, the ground like rock; and when it grew dark, he disappeared back into the shack. They brought rations to the captain like alms to an invalid or beggar. After all, no one knew if he was under arrest, or demoted, or even if he was still on the books. Suddenly, one morning, the gusting wind carried the clatter of an engine over the steppe. Then, from the sentry towers, they tried to make out what was crawling its way towards the settlement, but it was still hidden behind the slope of the steppe. Soldiers poured out of the guardhouse. They couldn't see anything yet, but the settlement came alive with the sound of shouting: 'They're coming! They're coming for Khabarov!' The captain sprang out of his shack; his face, covered in prickly stubble, shone. 'He's been waiting for this,' sighed Ilya Peregud, who was standing to one side by himself, doing his duty.

When the prison lorry at last showed itself – it looked like an ordinary bread lorry – for some reason it did not turn off into the barracks, but drove on towards the camp, carrying them all behind it in a crowd. It stopped by the camp entrance.

The escorts jumped to the ground – a pair of soldiers stifling yawns and a warrant officer hurrying them on.

It turned out the escort had other orders: to bring another batch from prison to the camp. The head of the escort had heard nothing about the captain's case. Agitated, Khabarov sought answers from the warrant officer: 'Why are they not coming to arrest me, then? Anyway, since when has there been a general back at regimental base?'

'That's right, they say a general is coming from Moscow to do an inspection. They're expecting him any day now, but he hasn't got there yet. And guess what, they've had another fire at the regiment. Yes, it broke out in the garage, everything inside went up . . . They saved five vehicles, no more, although of course those that were out elsewhere are still in service. Everyone's at each other's throats, looking for someone to blame for the fire. You see, there's so much cash, so much equipment that went up at once!' The young man in officer's epaulettes said his piece, becoming more relaxed. 'The general's coming slowly, so to speak, but now this has happened he'll take his time inspecting the regiment, that's for sure.'

At this, Khabarov turned excitedly towards him: 'My fellow countryman, do me a favour: if the general's going to be there, then I urgently need to get to the regiment. Would you drop me off nearby?' The other man agreed without hesitation. 'Get in, it makes no odds to me . . . Just not in the cab.'

'Ah, I'd ride on top, if need be! Wait for me, I'll go grab my things . . . ' Khabarov roused himself and dashed into the barracks. But when he'd got all his things together in a flash and sprung back out into the square, the Black Maria was already heading off into the distance. Something about the captain had unnerved the officer after all, and so they hadn't waited. Left behind, Khabarov made plans with Peregud: 'In the morning, I'll go to the regiment. I'll make it as far as Ugolpunkt, then hitch the rest of the way.'

Ilya was agreeing to all of it. 'Yes, you go. See that it all gets sorted out. Tell them there not to unleash the hounds. If need be, we'll say you ran off by yourself.' Then they sat together for a while, like they used to in the old days. They recalled everyone they had known, everyone they had served with, especially Vasil Velichko. The captain lay down to sleep in clean underwear on the bunk in his office – and would have missed his train, had Peregud not woken him as agreed, very early in the morning.

In the window were faint traces of light like smoke, and the long winter darkness. That night, the first frost had settled on the steppe. While the bitter cold was still some way off, the muddy roads had solidified. In the square, where the captain took his leave of Ilya, the previous day's footprints lay on the surface like potholes, while lumps of mud fallen from the men's boots had turned silver overnight; the potato field, too, had turned silver and hard.

The camp's narrow-gauge railway ran as far as the station halt at Stepnoi, through which, as with all the other far-flung halts, ran the main line to Ugolpunkt, the capital of this part of the steppe, and of the camps. The shunting engine always stood outside the gates of the camp zone, a little into the steppe, so that the *zeks* could not drive it away. At five o'clock in the morning, one of those camp-workers who had earned the freedom to go about unescorted shackled up the engine and drove it to Stepnoi. On the way there, it was empty; on the way back, it carried the new shift to replace the warders who had been on duty for the previous twenty-four hours. Khabarov had not had a chance to shave and spruce himself up the way he wanted, but time wouldn't wait: it was coming up to five o'clock. 'Off you go, then, off you go . . . ' repeated Ilya, staring at the ground. They said goodbye briefly, as if going their separate ways. But when Khabarov was already marching away from the gates, the warrior called out, 'Iva-a-an!'

'Wha-a-at?' echoed the captain, from afar.

'Ru-u-un! You-ou can ma-a-ake it! Run from the-e-em, follow your nose, don't come back, hide – I'll cover for you, I won't te-e-ell!'

Dawn was breaking over the steppe; the stark, swollen skies bobbed up from the night like a drowned man. The dawn was a dark blue, and cold: no sun, no clouds, no birds. Khabarov walked along the caterpillar-track ruts left by the camp tractors. The bit of breeze that was blowing past him caught in the cloth of his greatcoat, and set it rumbling and fluttering, gnawing at it like an angry dog. Khabarov climbed up onto the platform, which was open to the elements and rusting, and set himself down on an ammunition case. These had been dumped here by the dozen, so that you had something to sit your backside on along the way.

He looked at the Karabas he had left, seeing it quite clearly, through a stranger's eyes, and the image of the distant camp settlement moved him as though it were his own old photograph.

The trusty appeared – an old fellow with a wooden leg strapped to his stump with thick string. Once he had got out by himself, he skipped along almost mischievously, not like an invalid, but like a little boy. Before setting his railway train in motion, the old fellow gave the captain a hard stare, working out who this person was. Then he recognised him and so didn't start with any questions; instead, with preternatural calm, he skipped up into the driving compartment.

The engine began to puff as it dragged itself away from Karabas, which grew smaller and smaller, swallowed up by heaven and earth until it finally vanished from view. The sleepers beneath the rails had rotted, and it seemed that the rails were wobbling to and fro as though traced out by ice skates – here they bulged out, there they curved in and down and even rippled. The shunter skidded, shrieking, when its wheels jammed; here it bobbed and there it dipped as it went along the tracks.

In Stepnoi, the shift-workers were already waiting, numbed by the wind. Unnoticed by anyone, as though a stranger, the captain of Sixth Company jumped down from the platform and remained at the halt.

Such halts were spread along the branch line like weeds. A Kazakh emerges from the steppe, sticks his banner into the ground, or maybe just ties a horsetail to a saxaul tree, and there's your stop. Stepnoi, on the other hand, had been built more purposefully: the *zeks* of Karabas had built it for the ease of their warders. The structure resembled a barracks, but it was at least possible to shelter from the rain inside, plus they had furnished it to the best of their ability: there were benches and a stove. In its prime, the barracks had had a little extension built on, a shed and a co-operative, in which they traded with the Kazakhs, who brought furs and wool, and anything that they happened to make, into Stepnoi. In exchange they were offered primus stoves, logs and the like, and vodka.

When there were elections to the people's Soviets, a propaganda point would be set up in Stepnoi for the steppe-dwellers from the nearby shepherds' bases and other such nomad camps. They would get dressed up to the nines; clans and families would gather together, travelling on wagons and horses, learning the last five years' news from the propagandists. They would vote, but they wouldn't go so far as to poke their faces into the barracks. They would sit themselves down in the steppe around a big fire; they'd eat, drink, and then go their separate ways again. When the halt was burned down, they never finished rebuilding it. The camp-dwellers blamed the Kazakhs, but you may as well try and catch the wind in a field. However, between themselves, the prison authorities in Karabas knew that the halt had been burned down by the warders themselves when, returning from their shift, they had got stranded at Stepnoi. They had drunk too much, and when the night chill had clutched at their thin hides, they had there and then set light to the barracks. They kept themselves warm, and so escaped certain death.

Of all the structures at the halt, only the latrine had been spared. It lay close to the ground, for some reason, like a dug-out. Its walls were wattle and daub, in the Asiatic manner, with clumps of straw poking through the clay daub that held it all together instead of nails. The latrine roof had been swept away all the same, to be replaced by a bit of greasy khaki canvas that some practical-minded individual had stretched across.

With great tenacity, this structure thrust itself out of the earth to the height of a few inches – it was both a milestone and a station, not to mention plenty of other things. 'They could at least have planted some trees,' thought Khabarov, gloomily.

Suddenly, the halt became more cheery: out of the blue a few Kazakhs had appeared, plus a few of their women and children. They sat down, keeping a good distance from the captain. The Kazakh women sat in pairs, clearly mothers- and daughters-in-law, or even mothers and daughters. They were waiting for the train.

The young women were fair-skinned and slim, while the old women had skin like cured ham and were fat. They had three children with them, one of whom was ill, shivering with fever in a kind of papoose. They must have been taking him to Ugolpunkt, to the doctor there. They sat round the boy in silence, like a single family. An old woman, the oldest among them, wiped his sweating brow with her flabby hand from time to time. Yet the youngest of the women, who was most likely his mother, did not reach out to him, although her eyes were brimming with grief.

She was still very much a girl – fragile, flat-chested, with swollen pink lips and soft down beneath them.

The healthy children were clambering around in the ruins of the barracks, looking for nails in the ashes. Anxious, the grey old women called them back, but they either did not dare or did not wish to raise their voices against their future menfolk, and so they seemed instead to beseech them. Watching the steppe-dwellers, Khabarov was struck by the way Russian mothers would instead curse and swear at their own flesh and blood, and his gloom deepened.

And now, believe it or not, it turned out the diesel engine was being driven by a Russian woman! A strapping lass, she leaned out of the window as she brought her train, which consisted of three prison transport wagons and the same again of goods wagons laden with a rare selection of old crap, to a standstill at a platform way past the station halt. Going past, she cried: 'You'll have to get on like this, I won't back her up. Fucking hell, you can walk for all I care!' The servicemen ran for the carriages, while, not waiting to be asked, Khabarov snatched up the shouting Kazakh women's bundles, and together they ran to catch up – only it was difficult because of the little boy: carrying him, they couldn't keep up. Then the captain abandoned the bundles and, going back, took the little Kazakh from the old woman, who was struggling for breath. The fearful young Kazakh women stretched out their arms to the people on board and thus were lifted through the air and into the dark goods wagon that had been refitted to carry people. But the old women hanging onto the wagon wailed, scared that they might be forgotten. It was hard work dragging them on board – Khabarov got under their weighty behinds and shoved upwards, while from on board the goods wagon they tugged at their arms with all their might. From her engine the driver was yelling: 'I'd run over every last old woman!'

The train shuddered and set off, so that the captain had to leap into a wagon that was already moving. This he managed without any great danger to himself: the train wasn't powering ahead so much as waddling along the tracks, waggling its swollen hips from side to side like an old woman. Inside the wagon, the warmth was oppressive. The space was heated by coal, poured right in, in a great mound, and consumed bit by bit in an old barrel. There were benches nailed to the floor on which folk had huddled together in the smoky half-light. The captain could not make out any of them, and could only hear their loud breathing. From the corner of the workers' wagon, a rotten stink intermingled with the stuffiness – there, in the floor, a hole had been knocked through; daylight shone through it, filtered by a scanty piece of veneered board.

Khabarov shut his eyes, even though there was no point; but it seemed easier to bear like that. There were more stops, and everything happened just as at Stepnoi – people crowded onto the workers' wagons, the engine driver shouted at them, as if it wasn't the locomotive but she herself, harnessed to a barge-hauler's straps, who was dragging the wagons away from the platforms. And at each halt, each bare, wild halt, there would inevitably be a shithouse: wattle and daub or even wooden, with a roof or without, crooked, smeared with shit, with scratched sides: 'Brick Factory'; 'Sunray'; 'Karakul'; 'Pravdinskii'; '43rd Kilometre'. And so they formed a line, like guides, all the way to Ugolpunkt itself.

•

Once upon a time, at the place where this small town now stood, the steppe had just got on with life, but people in blue-edged uniforms had marched up, driving a crowd of convicts before them, and it was upon their bones that the town had been built. It was a town of coal mines and camps, although the coalfaces were soon deserted.

The train did not arrive at the actual station in Ugolpunkt, but came in to a siding. The sweating mass of people piled out into the cold. Khabarov fixed his eyes on his new godson, the little boy, and helped the Kazakh women carry him down and on to the station, where the local doctor was waiting to receive them. The women rewarded his labours with their bread, on top of which they gave him three roubles. The captain did not refuse their bread and other food – they would come in very handy for his onward journey – but he felt ashamed to accept them.

The station was a hub, with a marshalling yard, so Khabarov was not alone here as he had been at the halt. He looked at the tracks, strewn randomly over the ground, leading off in all directions; he listened to the shunters hooting; and he breathed the burnt air thrown out by the blackened trains as they passed through on their way from one far-flung place to another.

The Kazakhs mingled with the Russians, and there was a great shove of people like at a market. Baggage was piled up, and children, forgotten for the while, ran to and fro among it, playing games. When the local train came in, the crowd quietly carried the captain along into it; among these same people he sat down on a bench and fell asleep, surrounded by them all, as if at peace. He was roused by an old woman, in a carriage that was already empty. 'Now then, I'm an old fool and a sinner, my dear, I took you for dead, and you were only asleep . . . Heavens, but what a face you were pulling! Let me make the cross, for your sins. Here we are now, in Karaganda. Maybe you missed your stop? Anyway, keep well, I'll be off. Don't fall ill, now. Stay out of trouble.'

With the sign of the cross made over him, which for some reason upset him, Khabarov set forth into Karaganda, having slept so well that he could remember nothing. He'd had occasion to serve in this town. Remembering that he had deserted, he stepped up his pace, surprised as he recognised everything anew. The station was situated on the outskirts, as was the regimental base; as he drew nearer, so the captain's anxiety grew . . . Suddenly he remembered that he had not shaved nor had his hair cut as required, and so, remembering with relief the three roubles he had been given by the Kazakh women, he hurried off to the barber's; he was worried that he wouldn't find it in its old location, but there it was, still. They shaved him, gave him a crew-cut and sprayed him with eau-de-cologne at his own request, so that he would look his finest. His appearance became so impressive that they let this unknown captain into the regimental base without a pass; what's more, they even looked at him with respect as they breathed in the scent of his eau-de-cologne. Unhindered by anyone, the captain made his way into HQ . . . After a short while, yells and the sound of fighting could be heard from within; men fled, officers and soldiers alike, while a person, wheezing from the suffocating embrace he was held in, was dragged out of the entrance, all the while trying to tear himself free and get back into HQ. From the scrum came piteous shouts: 'He wanted to kill comrade Pobedov!' To all this was added yet more horror because the man stank of eau-de-cologne and was wheezing, as loud as he could: 'I'll kill him! I'll kill him!' Caught, as it were, at the scene of the crime, the evil-doer began to receive a beating, but then his assailants came to their senses: 'Take him off to the Special Department!'

6

A PASSION FOR ORDERS

Reveille in the sickbay happened later than in the barracks. The sickbay was managed by a military doctor with a foreign-sounding surname; it was his habits that set the rules here. A sergeant major roused the men from their beds before the doctor arrived, although he himself would hide in the storeroom and doze, waiting to find out what mood his boss was in that morning.

Relaxing after breakfast, which had been brought to him right in the ward, Skripitsyn set off to explore the sickbay, still holding his dirty crockery. He wanted to wander round, maybe eavesdrop on conversations, but the sickbay was full of the wildest people. The wards, which seemed just like gas chambers, were crammed with either Kalmyks or Kyrgyz, little earthenware figurines, wordless, quiet. This little tribe was huddled to the walls in the corridor, and everyone – there must have been about fifty mouths, you wouldn't have put it at any less – everyone was eating right there out of mess tins, ignoring everything around them, just hunched over their tins.

Wishing to be of use to the Special-Department agent, the sergeant major sprang towards Skripitsyn and led him out into the fresh air, clearing a way for him. Striking up a conversation with him about this black tribe, Skripitsyn's mind wandered around and about the sergeant major's simple replies. The more junior man explained that the rejects from every company had been brought to the sickbay. They couldn't serve on sentry duty, so it had been decided to send them off to the construction battalions in Baikonur and Semipalatinsk. 'They've been here at least a week, they've worn us all out, but they still haven't been sent on,' the sergeant major moaned.

Hearing him out, Skripitsyn passed him his dirty plate as if he had had plenty to eat and set straight off for the chief medic. When Skripitsyn promised the medical officer that he would send all these rejected human resources off that same day to their intended destination, the medic instantly cheered up, and assured the Special-Department agent that he would see to everything that was his responsibility without delay.

A man could only be discharged from the regiment if the adjutant signed him off. Ringing Degtiar and telling him, incidentally, that he was unwell, Skripitsyn reported with great feeling the existence of the spongers he had discovered by chance in the infirmary. Degtiar agreed with Skripitsyn's observations and, in an hour, at the adjutant's order, an old bloke appeared in the infirmary. He had been charged with sorting out train tickets, and he wanted a list with a headcount of the people he would be taking, so that he could get hold of supplies.

Meanwhile Skripitsyn had taken the medical officer to one side and whispered to him that the list for transportation had to include one more soldier: a private from the Special Department who had become unsuitable. The doctor demurred, saying it took more than a day just to have someone discharged from the sickbay. But Skripitsyn insisted and the medic gave way, and so Private Kolodin's documents, which he pieced together on the spot, were sent off via the same old bloke to Degtiar, who signed them all off, barely glancing at them.

They sounded lights-out in the regiment. Khabarov had yet to make his entrance, and Skripitsyn hadn't counted on the captain appearing immediately, nor had any reports from Karabas reached him. Added to which, Skripitsyn knew the colonel's habits; he knew that the colonel only had to put something off for him to forget about it straight away, since his tendency was to forget rather than to do.

Knocking at the Special-Department door, Skripitsyn roused Kolodin from his bunk and, not allowing him to come round, unsettled him by saying: 'They're taking some of those savages off to the division and you're going to help escort them. I gave my personal word. Be at the sickbay in the morning. Go on, don't let me down. It'll be a chance for you to wind down a bit, too; relax.'

His greatcoat had been cleaned and pressed by Sanka; it was ready and waiting for him, which Skripitsyn noted; he took it without a word.

In the morning, Sanka Kolodin did not find his boss in the sickbay, so could not say goodbye to him. This made him gloomy. However, the wild tribesfolk took Kolodin to be yet another boss: he was Russian, well built and had served his time. He had a sullen look on him and was dressed head to foot in new gear.

The old bloke tasked Sanka with getting the dry rations from the stores and making sure that all the greatcoats had their epaulettes torn off. Sanka did not rip off the epaulettes. In fact, he stayed aside as the tribesfolk were ordered to strip naked and prodded towards the shower room, although they had to wait while the keys were found. The medical officer was walking round and checking the rejects for signs of lice or rashes, striking out to mark crosses on some of the shaven temples. Then he shouted to his sergeant major, who was in charge of the knot of people: 'Vasia, my duck? The ones I put a cross on? They've gone septic! Give them a going-over with antiseptic liniment, but don't let them in the showers. Vasia, they haven't got lice, though. You can leave their underwear!'

The shower room was more like a utility room: barrels of paint and slaked lime were stored there. There was just enough space left to stand under the shower head: an old stewed-meat can had been soldered onto the end of an ordinary hooked tap and had holes punched through the bottom, and so they showered. In his boots and jodhpurs, deigning only to roll up the sleeves of his shirt, the sergeant major stood in the shower room while behind him icy water dribbled out of the tin; the jagged flows looked like iron swarf. The men went in single file to wash, the sergeant major checking that no one remained dry. He shoved through anyone who hesitated and formed a blockage, while trying not to get splashed himself. Into the passageway, where the men were turning numb with cold, he threw a single towel between all of them. And while they were rubbing themselves down, Kolodin and the old bloke began handing out underwear and uniforms. Through the doors of the sickbay could be seen the cunning, greedy visages of men who had run in from all over the base. In a flash, they had swapped anything worth having for their cast-offs.

But when the soldiers grew so bold as to start dragging the provisions out of their sacks, Kolodin put a stop to their marauding. He picked up a can of stewed beef that had rolled out and began treating the soldiers to it: some in the eye, others across the head, and drove them all away.

When the daft buggers had been lined up at the railway station, they grew boisterously happy, probably thinking they were to be sent home. They got themselves on the train quickly and efficiently. The old bloke was still threatening the drunk conductor to make sure the carriage entrances were locked up overnight, to which the latter agreed surprisingly easily, while Sanka had already started assigning shelves to the men, and taking their military belts off their greatcoats as a kind of passport to ensure they would not desert. It was a second-class citizen among trains, one of those that made unscheduled stops, that was driven onto sidings at night to make way for the express services, and that also stopped at every nameless station to take on more passengers. They didn't even serve the usual stinking tea, and there was nowhere to wash.

The old bloke grew silent on the journey. Kolodin, too, stayed wordless. By dusk, the train had made a good distance from Karaganda; all around the wild expanse of the steppe reached away. 'It's about time we ate something, or we'll forget,' said the old bloke, and Sanka heard him. He pulled out flasks of water, dry black bread and stewed meat from the sack he had been guarding, and began calling and otherwise summoning the men to get their food.

Once they had eaten, the rejects, who had been causing a racket from every shelf, grew tired and settled down to sleep. The old bloke was puzzled as to why they were sending Sanka, a bright, healthy soldier, off to kick the bucket in the construction battalion alongside the rest of them. He couldn't restrain his curiosity, and sat down alongside the Russian soldier. 'Can't you sleep? Do you know, for instance, where they're sending you?'

'Don't you mix me up with them,' replied Kolodin. The old bloke took offence: 'Hey listen, you, they're sending you off to serve in Baikonur, in a construction battalion. You'll be munching on radiation. So you really are a fool, after all.' He hadn't meant to blurt out the secret, but he had wanted to appear important and needed, and he also thought that he wasn't giving away anything he shouldn't, just leaving an impression. 'I take you there and then I come back. It's not the first time I've done this trip. How come you ended up here? How come the army didn't work out for a strapping lad like you?' Kolodin said nothing. The old bloke didn't feel like speaking to him any more.

At one point, in the dead of night, when the carriage, piled to the ceiling with motionless bodies, was barely moving, Kolodin cloaked himself in his greatcoat and began to make his way towards the door, taking nothing with him. He stepped through this scrapyard of bodies with difficulty, emerging and pitching up in the doorway, cold, clean, and alive. But the immeasurable length of the black steppe surface was broken by the lights of an unknown station. The train, hauling itself along and rattling its metallic vertebrae, was slowly pulling alongside a bit of inhabited land. Solitary yells rang out, some faint, others more distinct. Sanka could see a little brick-built station, neatly whitewashed, resembling a peasant hut. The night was thick with people hustling to and fro. Sack-like shadows had begun to quiver in puffs of illuminated dust. Along the sides of the virtually motionless wagons rained a tiny hailstorm: people were running along the train, tapping on the wagons as they went, looking for any that were unlocked or without conductors.

The pause began to feel oppressively drawn-out, as though just ahead of the train's dumb head, the iron rails had been torn up. Suddenly, a Kazakh climbed up into the doorway that Sanka was sitting in, a swarthy man, sweating from his run alongside the carriages. He took fright at the apparition of this huge soldier and froze on the footplate, muttering in Kazakh, 'It's setting off, it's setting off...' Kolodin moved towards him, reaching out to help, but the Kazakh jumped down in fear and disappeared into the darkness. With no time to think it over, as though he had lost his balance, Sanka tore down after him and found himself on hard, solid ground. His head span. He staggered, gulping down gusts of air made cold by the wind, and did not notice that the wagon behind him had set off and was moving in a long line of others that looked just like it.

The little station building lay there in its own bright spot, empty of people, while the carriages went on and on, leaving behind a lifeless steppe, as though carrying off its last inhabitants. And Kolodin was left alone, not yet realising his predicament. All his tobacco had been used up. His identity documents were still in their little official case, along with the sack that contained the entire extent of that time-served soldier's property.

Having breathed unfettered air to the point of breakdown, Kolodin felt an ominous void inside himself. It was this that drew him towards the little station, from the darkness towards the light. The whitewashed hut was surrounded by a flexible fence woven from the boughs of a steppe shrub. Smoke hung over the roof, and windows goggled out from the walls at regular intervals just above ground level. The building itself was squat, as though it had been flattened. The yard smelt of dung bricks, and dogs lay around on the cold ground. As soon as Sanka stepped inside the fence, they roused themselves and began to howl, although they shrank from attacking. These curs were more likely strays than servants of the people that owned the place.

Kolodin stepped back, but the dogs suddenly fell quiet and turned towards a well-fed, loosely dressed man who had jumped angrily out onto the porch. 'Who's carrying on out there?' he roared, not coming down. Sanka weighed the matter up, waiting. The Kazakh, though, suddenly making out the army greatcoat and fur hat, called again, this time more cautiously: '*Ai*, Warrior, where are you going, and where have you come from?'

'I got left behind by the train, I need to get to Karaganda,' responded Kolodin, growing scared. 'I could do with knowing when the train to Karaganda will be.'

'So what was your rank, what was your unit?' asked the Kazakh, delaying; he hadn't believed this masterless soldier from the word go.

'I'm from the Karaganda escort . . . '

'Oi, a soldier! Good, a soldier! Come in 'ere, come in . . . Give me your document, 'kay?' It was plain to see that the Kazakh was in charge of this station lost out in the steppe; he was an elderly bloke who'd grown a pot belly, a moustache and a beard that looked like a hairy fist. His face was round and cake-like, but his eyes were dark and caustic. You wouldn't have taken him for anything other than Kazakh. But still less would you have taken him for anything other than the pettiest of petty officials. Born to be light and straightforward, his face had swollen into crude, impudent features. His uniform jacket was too tight for his stout frame and swollen gizzard, while his wide uniform trousers were tucked into cowhide officers' boots. On top of his head, as though on a nail, perched a faded peaked cap with a brand-new red star; this also seemed to have been taken from someone else's swede. 'My ID, my papers, they're still on the train. I haven't got anything, I left it all there . . . ' Sanka said, as though for the record; he hung his head.

'*Ai*, that's bad! Left behind, were you?' A little uneasy, given that he hardly came up to this soldier's chest, the stationmaster walked around him, looking him over and patting him; either he was marvelling at the soldier's bear-like build, or he was secretly searching him and judging what would be the best side to tackle him from. '*Ai, batyr*, there'll be no Karaganda for a long, long time . . . ' he sang out, as he circled around the soldier.

'So what am I to do, father?'

'You get on the train tomorrow! I give you a ticket, I give you something to eat. I give you everything. Balakaev admire the army. Balakaev in charge here. Left behind, were you?'

'I told you, I need to get to Karaganda . . . '

'*Ai*, Karaganda-manda. Not for a long time yet. Listen, I give you a ticket tomorrow. All right? You come in, though. Balakaev pour vodka.'

They walked into this place that was half-station and half-dwelling, finding themselves immediately in a spacious, scruffy changing room with a row of bare government-issue benches; the air inside was grey from the tobacco smoke it had absorbed. Further off stretched only an empty, draughty passage, in the gloom of which Kolodin thought he saw a chain of doors, set almost flush into the wall. It was warm in the passage, and it smelt of frying, boiling and laundry. The room they came into from the yard was for official use, but it was also lived in, to a certain extent. On the wall, as in every boss's office, there hung a portrait of Lenin – dome-headed, narrow-eyed, looking like a Kazakh. There was also a portrait of comrade Brezhnev, in which he was depicted as still youthful, resilient and, once again, almost incontrovertibly resembling a Kazakh. Balakaev, as he had called himself, hurried to seat the wary soldier at the desk, clearing its surface of documents and other litter. He was in two minds whether to leave the soldier alone, and so simply looked into the passage, shouting impatiently in Kazakh: 'Wife, get up, you stupid cow. Bring me vodka and something to eat, and look lively!' Meanwhile he hurriedly reassured the soldier with an oily smile. 'I call my wife. We eat, drink . . . ' And again he yelled into the passage: 'Look lively! *Ai*, you stupid cow!' He sat down, wheezing, to get his breath back. Shortly after, an old woman, so tired as to seem almost dead on her feet, noiselessly appeared in the room, holding a little, opaque green bottle and a wooden bowl containing pieces of mutton flesh that had been fried to go with the drink. Noticing the soldier, the old woman shrank back and sprang to her husband in fright. 'Wife mine, idiot mine . . . ' The Kazakh pulled a face at Kolodin and continued speaking in Kazakh, not changing his sickly sweet, oily expression: 'You idiot, keep quiet . . . He's a deserter, we'll have to inform the department once he's got drunk.'

'Let him be . . . ' the old woman said, quietly.

'He's come to the wrong guy for that!' barked the Kazakh, not taking his now chill gaze from his wife, and then he burst out laughing: '*Ai*, the fool! She thought the wars were carrying me away! Och, och. Pour vodka, wife, Balakaev makes friend with guest.'

Sanka also laughed, to keep in with his kind host. The Kazakh poured him a glass and nudged the mutton closer to him: 'Let's drink for our army!' Kolodin was embarrassed just to grab the meat, so he drank, each time rejoicing that this other kindly soul was pouring refills so often, so that he could chase them down simply and easily with the mutton, which was really tasty. He was a hopeless drinker. Unused to vodka, he got a skinful more quickly than he got his stomach full.

The Kazakh grew weary of the young lad, who had turned wild: he was banging his fist on the table and demanding more vodka. He dragged the soldier's great-coat from him and passed it to his wife on the sly. He dragged Sanka himself off into a dark store cupboard and tipped him onto some sacks, bolting the door.

It was searingly cold in the cupboard. From his sprawling position on the sacks, Kolodin obstinately drew himself upright and made for freedom, away out of the damp and the dark, but he was stymied by the bolts. 'Open up, father, I feel dreadful!' He hammered on the door, growing scared of the place. Just the other side of the door, the Kazakh called out evilly, 'Sit still, Sit still! Here, Balakaev the boss.'

'Open up!'

'Sit quiet, deserter. Listen, for you is prison.'

'You bastard! Open up, or else I'll break it down!'

'Listen, Balakaev have gun, will shoot!'

The Kazakh was trying to scare the deserter, but he had no illusions about the strength of the bolts. And when the door began to splinter under this wrathful, bear-like onslaught, launched by a man who apparently had nothing left to lose, Balakaev fled to safety, in disarray. After long, despairing attempts, Sanka broke through the door. Seeing that there was neither gun nor Kazakh on guard, he set off determinedly, aiming for the outside, but remembering something, he turned back, enraged still further, in search of his stolen greatcoat. Finding no trace of it in the room where they had been drinking, Kolodin made out an axe in the corner and picked it up, in recollection of the unobtrusive doors in that shadowy passage, behind one of which, perhaps, the Kazakh might have hidden. He broke one down with the axe, but behind it was nothing more than railway-workers' lanterns and tools. The next door he sent flying open with one blow:

in the little room behind, in the middle of bare, washed-down walls, a feeble lightbulb smouldered on its flex, illuminating children asleep on sagging government-issue bunks. Among them, among her own children, the stationmaster's old woman was keening quietly to herself, her knobbly knees planted firmly into the floor. She couldn't cover all her sons and daughters with her own body, so she threw herself at the feet of the soldier. 'Where's my greatcoat? Hand it over!' croaked Kolodin, brandishing the axe in the dim light. 'The coat, the coat, or I'll kill them all, you bitch!'

At this, the children woke, and Sanka, left for a moment by the old woman who had shot off to fetch his coat, looked venomously at them; at the mere sight of him, they began wailing and weeping. As soon as he got his property back, Sanka dropped the hefty axe on the spot. He made his way rapidly out of the house, then ran along the sleepers that vanished into the distance, going, as far as he could tell, back: back to distant, unattainable Karaganda.

It seemed to Sanka Kolodin that he was being chased. He clearly heard both the howl of dogs and the clatter of boots in the steppe night. He fell, rose, and again exerted every sinew. Until he fell off the tracks . . . Laying on his back until he recovered, the escapee scrambled onto all fours but, suddenly, clutching at his throat, he sank face down onto the stony ground in a surprise fit of asphyxiation, worse than any pain. Sanka swelled up, and his horror-stricken eyes, streaming with tears, nearly burst out of their sockets. And just at that moment, when it seemed he would surely rupture, from his throat there came a whistle, needle-thin; and then the remnants of what he had eaten without looking, washed down with the stationmaster's vodka, came flying up. Afterwards, Kolodin drew a breath, like an infant who had just emerged from its mother's belly, and crawled away, fearing to look at the puddle of vomit that had nearly choked him.

There was no sound of any pursuit to be heard. And Sanka could not see the lights of the station in the distance . . . He felt at ease, even though he did not know why he was still alive.

The deserter was pulled out of this puppyish oblivion by the rumble of a locomotive; first one train and then another, heading in different directions, were dragging themselves along above him.

The tracks at this point ran tight along a curving ridge, and the cautious engine-drivers bridled their steel horses, so as not to topple over sideways at full speed.

Creeping up to the tracks, Kolodin hid, and waited for a goods train. The one that came was made up of empty coal trucks. Letting the engine pass far ahead, he leapt up onto the embankment and ran level with the shaking trucks, trying to catch hold of their sheer, deeply gouged sides. The wagons were inching away, but suddenly there was a flash of light and he saw shackles hanging down. He grabbed at them and was instantly dragged off the embankment, dangling in dumb panic, although the wagons were still moving. As petrified as ever, Sanka jerked his way up the shackles and tumbled over the screeching side, falling into the very bottom of the truck, which was strewn with coal. Instead of an impact, he experienced great relief, as though both pain and fear had been knocked out of him. Sprawling, listening to the coal skittering along the hollow iron truckbed, he looked up at the iridescent starry night, sparkling like a goldmine. It was arrayed above the warped sides of the coal truck, seemingly returning secretly from a journey to unknown parts.

The train stopped at a station while Sanka was asleep. A railwayman made his way aboard the wagon and shouted, with a guffaw: 'Come on then, get up, you lousy fucker! You fleeing from the front? Who the hell are you?' The deserter crawled into a corner and sat dumbly quiet. 'Don't stay quiet!' The railwayman was upset. 'Come on, tell me your tale, I love this stuff . . . I have all the luck: the useless gits always turn up on my shift. Run away, then, have you? What are you staying quiet for? Look, don't stay quiet, or I'll turn you in, you hear? Maybe I've got a soft spot for runners. Maybe I did a bit of time for it myself.'

'I need to get to Karaganda,' said Sanka.

'We've got our own Karaganda here, as far as you're concerned.'

Chuckling, the railwayman arrested the soldier and dragged him off. Passing under trains of goods vans that stretched for kilometres, they made their slow way to the depot.

Sanka had no idea which way to run in this clanking metal forest, so he obediently followed after the railwayman, who was asking him questions as gleefully as if he had started rooting around in Sanka's very innards.

At the depot, the work team cheerfully joined in, drinking and chasing it down with obscenities: a real rabble. 'His mummy's in Karaganda, a dear old lady. He's his dear old mum's first and last child, bugger me if all her hopes aren't placed on him. He's running from the construction battalion, he's running for liberty! Well I've grown to love him, he's like a brother to me now. Look, I'd spill blood for him. Brothers, Fedulych, what should we do, then? Well, it was me that found him!'

The man to whom the team leader had appealed asked without looking at him, 'Is it true, then, all that bollocks about your mother this windbag was spouting?'

Kolodin said without hesitation, 'It's true.'

The foreman chewed this over a little in silence, then expressed surprise. 'Why's he got up? There's loads of grub, still, and he's standing up.' Kolodin sat down on a crate with the entire team. They passed him a link of smoked sausage, curled round like a mongrel's tail and with the same sort of red, crimped arsehole; they passed some bread in his direction, too. Starving, he set about devouring it all, which cheered the railwaymen. Then, as the team began to disperse, without saying farewell to the escapee – it was as though he did not exist – the foreman explained to Kolodin with drunken forcefulness that he was in Shakhtinsk, where there was nowhere to hide, just mines and the rail depot. 'You need to get yourself to Karaganda and once you're there you'll figure out where to head for.' He took it upon himself to guide Sanka to the mine, and set him on the bus that, as it happened, took the shift-workers from the mine to Karaganda itself. 'You sit quiet and you'll make it there.'

The folk from the mine, as opposed to the railway-men, were soberer and stronger. They briskly took the deserting soldier in hand. Not bothering to ask, they stripped all the obvious government-issue gear from him, apart from his underpants. One gave up some trousers, another a pair of worn-out boots, or a spare, faded shirt; they did what they could. These men, covered head-to-toe in coal dust, all looked the same – like Africans, he thought, or perhaps just devils. They passed Sanka along a human chain, instantly forgetting him once he had passed from their hands. At its end they put him in the miners' bus which would take him right to Karaganda.

The bus set Sanka down in a quiet spot, well away from any police patrols, where Karaganda was full of well-built miners' huts with yards containing old orchards which stood dark and silent at this time of year.

In the not quite two full days that had passed since Skripitsyn had sent Kolodin away from the regiment, the investigator had completely forgotten about his acolyte.

He was spending his nights in the Special Department. Late in the evening, he heard footsteps outside his door. In fright, he tore himself away from the documents that he'd been up so late reading and headed off in the direction of the footsteps, but he could not see anyone. The dark and the cold that poured in as soon as he opened the door pressed unpleasantly on the investigator standing on the threshold. He slammed the door shut, and went as far as locking it. But he hadn't even managed to get back to his desk in the office before he heard steps again, yet more clearly, and louder. Unhesitatingly, the Special-Department agent hurried to catch up with whoever it was.

Plunging headlong a few metres into the darkness, he ran into a man who he dragged into a dead end, at which point he recognised his acolyte, although he had no wish to believe that this dead man walking was back in his life. 'Hello, comrade Senior Warrant Officer . . . '

Skripitsyn fixed his eyes, sharp as shards of glass, onto him. 'Where have you come from?' Have you been seen on the base? Speak!' Unable to bear it any more, Kolodin clasped the hissing throat of his boss tightly in his hands, which looked as red as if they had been boiled. The acolyte was throttling the Special-Department agent, staring at him madly, seemingly trying with all his might to understand something. Either crying or howling softly, he would let go slightly of his croaking boss, then begin choking him again, until he suddenly turned and ran.

Skripitsyn's first impulse was to rouse the whole regiment there and then and place them on alert, but by the time he had got to the phone the Special-Department agent had thought better of ringing the guardhouse, so he ran off in search of the deserter himself. The sleepy sentries he bumped into in the darkness made out the head of the Special Department through bleary eyes, seeing nothing suspicious in his nocturnal zeal. At one point, he sensed something hidden in the dark: alive, and dangerous. This was at the lorry park. Skripitsyn remembered that from time to time Sanka had passed the night there, in his vehicle. However, even here, everything was calm at the sentry posts. The sentry was silent, pacing up and down by the gate. The notion that Kolodin had managed to escape from the environs of the base into the town heartened Skripitsyn, and he returned to the Special Department, ultimately deciding to keep everything that had happened that night a secret. As he saw it, the deserter had only two options left: to run into a patrol in the town, or to vanish in some unknown direction, but again, only as far as the first policeman or military patrol. After that, the usual court hearing, which would tie up all the loose ends.

A fire broke out at dawn – a vehicle was burning: the head of the Special Department's personal transport. It would have been in the power of the men at the sentry posts to stop the fire consuming the other vehicles, had they not seen, as they ran up with fire extinguishers, that there was a huge figure in the fire, from whom, it seemed, the very heat was streaming. He was the image of flame made flesh. He was shouting something through the roar of the fire and holding onto the blazing steering wheel with his burning hands. This sight scared them so much that they recoiled, pitiful and overwhelmed; they could only watch the fire's glow helplessly. Time was lost. By the time the alarm was raised on the base, the rank of vehicles was engulfed in a huge blaze. Fuel tanks exploded. It was impossible to approach the machinery. By morning, though, the lorry park at the Karaganda regimental base had burned itself out. The fire brigade had been pouring on water from a distance, but they still managed to shield the barracks and to win back several garages.

At the crack of dawn they dragged Fyodor Fyodorovich Pobedov from his warm bed and took him to the base in a prison van, like a common thief, because they were no longer able to send his personal car to fetch him. Who knows what was going through his mind as he jolted around in the back of the van, refusing to believe in any fire – was he to be purged? Shaken, red-eyed and tearful, the colonel set about deciding who to find guilty and who to hold accountable. They hurriedly formed the soldiers up on the square and spent a long time over the roll-call, checking against the lists. It turned out, though, that there was no one missing from the ranks of warrant officers and soldiers. So it was deduced that the man who died in the fire hadn't been serving in the regiment, but had broken in from outside. The sentries testified that they had encountered the unknown person while he was still alive, and that this mystery man had not called for help nor made any attempt to escape the fire, but rather had determinedly sat within it. So it transpired that this unknown man had perhaps even broken into the base with the aim of burning it down. Pobedov wanted to hide in his office, as was his wont, to sit a while and catch his breath. But yet again an emergency was reported: a desertion in the regiment. A soldier had, without authorisation, left his detachment on the way to a new place of service. It was a former private in the Special Department: one Kolodin, Aleksandr.

Furious, the colonel pictured how all this might have happened. He realised suddenly that the fire in the lorry park had also started with the Special Department; that is, with Skripitsyn's vehicle. And then he remembered that Skripitsyn had for some reason been among the first on the scene of the fire; that is, he had been on the base at dawn, as though he had been waiting for it to catch fire. Mind you, the vehicle could have caught fire by accident, and it would have been stupid to set fire to it and then parade about in full view. So if he had been awake until dawn, that was in fact a good thing; it meant he was putting the hours in. Added to which, as regards the soldier from the Special Department, the personnel officer reported that Skripitsyn had good reason to rid the regiment of him on the quiet: this soldier had been raped in one of the steppe companies by his fellow soldiers, non-Russians to a man, but so as to avoid scandal, the case had not been allowed to proceed. Finding it difficult to understand what was unfolding around him, Pobedov nonetheless realised that for various reasons the surname of the Special-Department head was flashing in his mind.

'Another fire? You know what, that's no accident. Proof, now, of course you won't prove anything. Both that time and this he wrote everything off, all the t's were crossed and the i's dotted. But it's time to act!'

And so, step by step, Fyodor Fyodorovich edged towards the idea that it was time to get rid of Skripitsyn, one way or another. And the colonel was already raising his voice and demanding Skripitsyn's presence, the sabo-teur. When the latter did present himself, stooping and downcast, the colonel waxed even more wroth, as if he did not want Skripitsyn to begin offering excuses. Yet Skrip-itsyn made no attempt to reply, remaining obediently silent. He stayed silent and imperturbable all the while, and even when the colonel finished by shouting, 'Gather your odds and sods together because, you little piece of shit, tomorrow you'll be marching off to serve somewhere out in the steppe!', he still said nothing in response.

The next day, Skripitsyn turned up for duty earlier than usual. The colonel put a call in to Skripitsyn equally early. 'Haven't you cleared off, yet?'

'Are you afraid, Fyodor Fyodorovich? Do you think I will run away?'

'Are you still poking fun at me? At the regimental commander? Gah! I've put up with you for a long time. A very long time . . . Do you know where I'm sending you? To Balkhash. You'll be chewing on copper.'

'And what if, for the sake of honesty, I reveal all the truth about you that Smershevich had locked away in his cabinets?'

'Ah. You piece of shit! You'd do that after all the kindness I've shown you? You're out of your depth, now. Mind you don't shit yourself. I'll have you up in court. In court!'

'Now, now. There won't be any court without you, Fyodor Fyodorovich. After all, you're the biggest criminal in the regiment!'

The colonel hung up. Skripitsyn meanwhile thought to himself, not without a certain pleasure, that the old git would have strung himself up by his own tie if he ever found out or could understand the whole truth. And it even occurred to Skripitsyn to tell them all about Sanka, just to see the looks on their faces when they found out that there hadn't been any sabotage. They simply wouldn't believe it! They wouldn't want to believe it. Taking a sheet of paper, he set about writing a dispatch: his resignation from the service. He took so long writing it that he lost track and started thinking about other things. Just then, a crowd of excited people burst into the Special Department, dragging what was either a person or a mannequin. 'Take this one in, he was about to shoot the regimental commander!'

As Ivan Yakovlevich Khabarov was coming to his senses, having been handed over to the Special Department, Skripitsyn tidied up a little in his office, which had become rather neglected. And although it had been his first meeting with the captain that had set all his future prospects crumbling to ashes, the crooked warrant officer looked at Khabarov with vacant indifference. If anything could have perplexed Skripitsyn after all this, it was the news that the captain had made an attempt on the regimental commander's life. Was Fyodor Fyodorovich so scared that he imagined the captain had intended to kill him? Or was this sorry excuse for a captain so enraged that he really had made the attempt? Yet his pistol was still under lock and key in Skripitsyn's safe; there was no pistol, so where had all this excitement come from?

Sensing the possibility of some kind of way out, although it still wasn't clear even to him exactly what, the Special-Department agent began their conversation. 'Well, then, did you decide to greet your dear father, Pobedov that is, with bread and salt? Did you offer him any? You just hang on in there . . . '

'You're dogs, the lot of you . . . One big gang, it seems.' Khabarov groaned, not wanting to understand anything.

'You swear about it, go on. That means you're still alive! It's just that you and I have nothing to share. I still wanted to help you, back in Karabas. Come on, what are you pulling faces for? After all, I've also got one foot in the grave that Pobedov has dug for me.'

'I'd kill him . . . ' affirmed the captain, and Skripitsyn shuddered. He waved away the soldier who had brought Khabarov in, and set about the captain himself. 'It's too soon to give in. Two honest people, that's a force to be reckoned with. It's good that you've understood who your friends are, and your enemies. I was gradually getting closer to this Pobedov, gathering evidence and facts;

I was working as hard as I could. But you wouldn't give me any testimony. There was no other option left . . . '

Shaken by this news, Khabarov raised his head, done over by the other officers' boots, and the lopsided warrant officer was amazed to see bright shining tears were rolling down from Khabarov's swollen eyes. 'Oh, why didn't you say so right away? I'd have spoken up!'

'Bit late for that now . . . ' said Skripitsyn. Looking away, he pushed the pistol towards the captain. 'Take this. It's yours . . . Leave, while you still can. Get away.'

'Please forgive me, dear comrade,' muttered Khabarov, taking the pistol and not knowing where to put it, once lost and now found.

The captain rose in silence and moved off, limping somehow crabwise, shoving the pistol into his greatcoat pocket while not removing his hands, as though keeping them warm. 'You look after the potatoes as best you can. Look after them!' And that was how they parted.

Khabarov had intended to stick to their arrangement and he would have made himself scarce, just as he had promised Skripitsyn, if only he hadn't bumped right into one of his oldest acquaintances, a completely insignificant sergeant major whom he had been friends with when they served alongside each other years back. Seeing his sorry appearance – and disapproving – the sergeant major did not want to let Khabarov leave. He was one of the storesmen, and Khabarov could not say no to him, on top of which he was experiencing an incomprehensible sense of gloom.

While they were having a drink and a bite to eat, Skripitsyn came to the end of his tether over the captain: pacing up and down while they got drunk, he thought with irritation that every impulse these people had, even the most unstoppable, would come to nothing. They burn up, smoke rises from them, and nothing is left but charcoal.

'Ah, that one wouldn't hurt a fly . . . ' he concluded gloomily, faltering at last. No longer able to hold back, he burst into the stores to kick the captain out of the room in which he seemed to have got stuck.

An unfamiliar lorry was spluttering by the regimental gates, waiting to be sent on its way. Skripitsyn jumped up onto the running board. 'Where are you headed?'

'I'm for Dolinka,' came the reply from inside.

'Right, well, take a passenger, you can drop him off at Sixth Company.'

'I'm not allowed, I've got cargo.'

'Do you know who you're speaking to? The head of the Special Department, that's who!'

'Well, there are plenty of bosses on the base, but I've got my own boss.'

'You'll take him, or I won't let you go!'

'I might be persuaded, three ought to cover it . . . ' Skripitsyn amenably scraped together three roubles.

After standing and waiting until the lorry had passed through the gates, Skripitsyn dolefully and indifferently went back to his office to finish writing his resignation. It was peaceful on the base, but he hardly had time to be surprised by this peace when some agitated officer ran determinedly out of HQ and, throwing open his arms just like they were wings, shouted out as he ran past, 'The regimental commander's having a cardiac! The commander's dying!' This harbinger flew into the sickbay and, before Skripitsyn's very eyes, the medical officer and an orderly ran for HQ. Meanwhile, having accomplished his objective, and still uneasy, the officer began wandering across the lifeless square. From God knows where, people began thronging towards him. Hurriedly, his words tripping over each other, he informed them: 'His heart gave out, an arrest; when he fell, he hit his head.' At this, Skripitsyn too headed into HQ.

The old colonel was lying flat on a strip of carpet on the floor of his office. Skripitsyn crossed over to the body, driving away the gawkers, clerks and other small fry who were just happy to have caught a glimpse. In the office there were the medical officer, Sokolskii, and Petr Valerianovich Degtiar. There was also a fat, weeping clerk, on whose knees the colonel's head was resting.

Skripitsyn could not bear the silence. 'Is he dead?' They were all convulsed with grief. Who knows what might have happened had he put it differently: 'Is he alive?'

Only the medical officer responded, saying clearly, 'Fyodor Fyodorovich has overdone it. His heart is not tireless. We'll build him back up.' His words liberated those present in the room; the colonel, however, did not so much as flutter his blueish eyelids, although Skripitsyn could by now clearly see that his chest was still rising and falling.

After a while, the doctors summoned from the hospital appeared. They were greeted with relief, as though the burden of responsibility had been lifted. Sokolskii insisted that he be allowed to accompany the regimental commander to the hospital. Perhaps he assumed that he would do everything to save the colonel's life, in contrast to the others.

Left alone together in the now-deserted anteroom, Skripitsyn and Degtiar began an unwilling conversation. Degtiar controlled himself: 'I know the colonel had raised the question of your discharge from the service if you were to refuse to serve in Balkhash. I did not agree with him. Personally, I respect you, Anatolii, but make your decision. I will have to carry out the order.'

'The comrade Colonel's like a drunkard: whatever's in his head gets blurted out of his mouth,' replied Skripitsyn, crudely. 'What you don't know is what he says about you.' Degtiar turned a deep shade of red, but stayed quiet. His unthinking steadfastness annoyed Skripitsyn. 'He used to say that your head was just like your you-know-what parts; that with a head like that you must not command the regiment, and this was about you, who's a thousand times better than he is.' Degtiar barked, 'Drop it, Anatolii, everything will be all right.'

'All right for who, though, Petr Valerianovich? Pobedov is hounding me. And then he will hound you. He's such a little tyrant that soon his suspicions will fall on you, too.'

'I can delay his order while Pobedov is away from the regiment. That's all I can do for you.'

Skripitsyn had not expected such decisiveness from the cautious Degtiar, and fell quiet, leaving Petr Valerianovich to his own thoughts.

7

THE WHOLE TRUTH

When the lorry turned off onto the frozen steppe road, it began to drizzle. The driver suddenly stopped; he had been seized by the need to piss. The big man had no desire to go outside. He twisted to one side and, hitching up his long-tailed greatcoat just like a skirt, sprayed out into the grey drizzle with a guffaw. 'Captain, look, it's pissing down!'

'That means we've got caught out, then. Think about it,' replied the captain. 'That's it, now, winter's here. In December the road will be blocked, you can be sure.'

'Lord, we've thrown the year away . . . Is this the last rain, captain?'

'That's your lot. Wait 'til spring for the next rain. You're on a wild goose chase there.'

'And will spring come around? What if, like they say, we get covered over in ice; we're fucked?'

'Quit talking rubbish . . . That can't ever happen.'

'Oh, I'm doomed!' This ginger, pock-marked galoot turned gloomy, jumping down out of the warm cab, which had suddenly become too small for him. He called out: 'This carriage won't go any further. You can go on foot, and I'm not giving those three roubles back. What's up, are you frightened?'

'You'll catch your death. What bollocks.'

'We only live once! Ugh, it sends shivers through me. It stings . . . Captain, see, I've got pissed on, all over! Climb out, we'll freshen up in this last autumn rain. See, it's like eau-de-cologne!'

'You're a nutter!'

'I'm a driver. Get your hands round a steering wheel, you'd find out, too. It's a free shower, see, and you've got a bit of soap on you. What's up, got lice?' Finally, the lorry set off. The soldier was pleased with his little escapade. Beforehand, he and the captain had travelled in silence, while now they were talking to each other, which made it easier for each of them to cope with the gloom of the kilometres stretched out ahead. Khabarov asked how well the servicemen lived in the Dolinka camp, and the ginger lad lied. And the captain almost certainly knew that the big lad was lying. Life there couldn't have been worse. However, Dolinka itself did not seem any closer thanks to these lies, but rather sped further and further away in his mind, to the edge of the earth.

The lorry was travelling up a wide incline, which was growing steeper the closer they got to the top. The road gained height up this slope like a drowning man striving for air, but the road was choking on it. Then, on the plateau that opened out, the steppe settlement of Karabas emerged. There were so many people crowding in the barracks square that they could be seen clearly even at this distance.

It seemed the whole settlement had turned out to greet the lorry, as if they had managed to get wind of the captain's arrival. The square was divided: a dozen fractious soldiers stood alongside Ilya Peregud, and a living wall of Kazakhs stood, not a crowd but a friendly family: a grey-haired elder in a shaggy cap and sheepskin coat, and behind him his indistinguishable sons, of different ages, behind whom in turn his grandsons were hiding. Their herd of horses was standing outside the gates.

When the lorry drove past, the horses jostled one another, hitting out with their bell-like rears. The Kazakhs too took fright, despite their own rather frightful appearance, complete with whips whose lash seemed to sting at the mere sight of them. The Kazakhs had joined the settlement in earlier times too; it was never clear from where. Sometimes one would lose his way, drunk, and they'd leave him to spend the night there. Sometimes, they came with invitations to hunt in the steppe, because the servicemen had weapons, even if they were only government-issue ones. More often, it was the little rascals among them who carried on their own trade with the soldiers: they trafficked the local strain of marijuana and also exchanged well-made, rare things for the cheap knock-offs of the camp, which every soldier saved up for this purpose. The older ones particularly valued planks, metal and, most of all, nails. They would barter these for foodstuffs. However, most expensive of all were the vicious camp guard dogs' pups, which the Kazakhs would exchange for sheep.

Surprised by nothing, Peregud presented a mighty figure, standing on his two feet like some cast-iron monument, and at Captain Khabarov's descent to the earth, with mournful, downcast eyes, greener than tarnished brass, he said, to no one in particular, 'So, from that world to this.' Only the Kazakhs seemed more certain, and more angry, as they recognised the captain of the steppe. Khabarov stood, upset, by the lorry. 'Bloody hell . . . What's happened now?'

'You what?' Ilya said reluctantly to the captain. 'Don't you know? You're lying, you must know.'

The Kazakhs were eavesdropping on the servicemen's conversation, and it seemed to them that the warrior with the topknot was trying to persuade his commander to confess, while the other one was being obstinate. Hearing talk of lying, the old man broke in on them, angrily: 'My family don't lie! Oman found it. The potatoes died in the steppe. Oman found it. He knows!'

'Ilya, son of a bitch, wake up. What's this old man going on about?'

'What's to tell?' said Peregud, in a voice made quiet by exhaustion. He spent a long time beating about the bush, but finally decided to spit it out. 'Turns out, there's none left. No potatoes, that is.' The Kazakhs as one reached

for their whips and pressed in on the captain as he
snatched hold of their elder: 'Did you see these potatoes
with your own eyes? That can't be possible, how can you
not understand? I don't believe it, you're lying . . . ' The
elder, without fear but with some strength, pushed the
captain away from him.

Having hung around long enough for them to
demand the use of his lorry, the big ginger-haired lad
bitterly rued the moment that he had stopped in the
settlement. He swore at the captain, but the latter climbed
into the cab of his own accord and stared at him, so that
the ginger lad had no option but to start up the engine.
The elder, who had decided to show them the place in
question after all, whooped at two of his kinsfolk, who
obediently climbed into the back of the lorry, while he
sat next to the captain in the cab, which was a novelty
to him. On the way, they did not exchange a single word,
each man quite alone beside the other. The Kazakh stared
out at the steppe, noting each bend and how far they
had travelled. His features were collected; stone-like, his
expression did not change. He was enjoying travelling
in the lorry, which led him to assume a dignified air.
The elder's determination was beginning to convince
Khabarov, and he started glancing at him more and more
often, his spirits falling.

Wordlessly, the elder led him off, far from the road,
the sides of which were already dissolving into the dusk.
Behind them, the elder's two kinsfolk stepped noisily
over the stony ground. The soldier stayed in his truck and

turned the engine off, so that all around became empty and still. There came a scent of something rotting, dissipated by the wind. The ground was rutted and covered in identical tyre prints made by the wheels of a lorry. An embankment of potatoes was staring at the frozen captain. It looked like a burial mound, and indeed it was a tomb. The elder looked at the hillock in surprise, prodding the captain: 'Look, look, are those your potatoes?' Khabarov bent down with difficulty, picked up a potato that may as well have been a cobblestone, and instantly dropped it. It banged hollowly onto the ground and did not roll. The Kazakh waited for the captain to say something. Then he touched him on the sleeve of his greatcoat, but it was as if there was no arm within. The old man was surprised. He muttered something and wandered off to the side, to his kinsfolk, who began whispering among themselves.

Suddenly, the lorry began rumbling mournfully in the steppe, scaring away the deathly hush. It was then that the captain broke down. It looked for all the world as though the man had reached complete collapse, and he fell prostrate. It hit him in the side, at first; he crumpled, although without a single groan, then sank to his knees and planted himself in the ground.

The Kazakhs ran and hid, but they could not bring themselves just to abandon him. When the lorry shot off in the opposite direction, away from the camp, the elder shouted something anguished after it, stamped his boots in anger, and huddled more warmly into his coat. The

Kazakhs had nothing to wait for. Standing motionless on that fatal spot, all they could do was freeze. However, taking pity on the captain, the elder unexpectedly bade them all to remain. The Kazakhs sat nearby on the ground, hunkering down right into it, which was how they sheltered from the wind. Meanwhile, the wind scoured about above their heads. Freezing through, the old man took up a song, lamenting under its plaintive drone, and when he grew tired, his kinsfolk sang in turn, while he listened.

Now, a group of anxious horsemen appeared in the night. The young men jumped headlong from their horses and dashed over to the weakened elder. He growled at them and gripped their arms for support. Once he had clambered onto the horse they had brought for him, regaining poise and power in the saddle, he sent some of the relatives who had hastened to find him off to fetch the captain from the mound. They hauled Khabarov to his feet. Seeing the horses pawing the ground, and their owners, he went without a murmur into the arms of the Kazakhs who had fetched him, and they tossed him onto the back of a horse whose rider was no more than a boy. Sensing that they were about to be loosed for a gallop, the horses started to prance; their shaggy muzzles with greedy, wide-open nostrils were lifted towards the steppe, towards the scent of the boundless black expanse. The elder was readying his stallion for the off, taking his leave of that ill-starred place without sentiment, but also without hurry. 'Though the potatoes was yours, Captain!' he exclaimed, as though he had worked it all out, and he set off on his way, not waiting for a response. The Kazakhs dispersed, whirled away by the wind, disappearing into the other side of the night. But the boy turned his horse in a circle and galloped hurriedly off towards the camp, as he had been commanded.

Catching the sound of solitary hoofbeats, Ilya strode out of the gate, crashing his vast frame into the approaching horse. The animal staggered back, afflicted by the scent of vodka, while Peregud held firm and did not stagger. The captain got down by himself, but collapsed again. The boy waved his lash to and fro so wildly that Ilya began to wonder whether the Kazakhs had left the captain unharmed. 'Are you alive, at least?' he called, and the captain came to again.

'They've rotted away. The potatoes have rotted away; they didn't even feed them to the pigs. Not even the worms got to eat them . . . They're all there, on the stones, they might as well be stones themselves.'

'What are you shedding tears over them for, Vania? The effort's a shame, that you broke your back for nothing, but that's your own fault. So don't do anything, don't believe anyone, just drink some vodka. We've run off into the steppe, we can run further still, go right round the earth. It's round, after all. Vania, cheer up, look: you're a long way from Moscow!'

It was as if this had seared the captain, so that he took a dislike to this drunken bullshitter who had laughed at his grief; although if Peregud had been laughing, it was in order to console the captain, to stop him giving up on life completely.

By falling out with the last person close to him and, what's more, making some effort to do so, at a single stroke the captain converted everything he had been accustomed to into something alien, which is what he had little by little begun to want. They were still standing side by side, so now Peregud accompanied him into the administrative office, staying assiduously by his side, imagining that he was leading home a lost friend. He even stayed in the office to sleep on the bare floor, although Khabarov himself tried to drive him away. Ilya would not budge, no matter how the other man tried to bundle him out. 'Be happy! Be happy!' The captain groaned from time to time, while Ilya lay still, only gulping from the bottle that was the one thing he had hugged to his chest with complete determination when Khabarov resolved to throw him out. Ilya had never seen his company commander so sober, so distant, like a block of ice. There was no trace of hangover in him, either, not even while he'd been in the truck. Peregud was perturbed that night; he kept waking up and dropping off, as if something was about to happen. Once he woke up and saw that the captain was writing and writing. Ilya felt sorry for him: 'So what's that you're writing, then? Leave off, drop it, or they'll come for you again . . . ' Khabarov turned round, frightened by the voice behind his back and, through his sleepiness, Ilya made out the captain's creased, tormented face, like a greasy rag – not remotely sober. Waking again, later, when it was already light, Ilya saw an empty desk and scrunched up paper scattered around, while the captain himself was sprawled on the bunk, asleep and snuffling. Ilya took off his boots and covered him with his greatcoat.

The captain opened his eyes at some dreary hour, very late in the day. The smell of liquor was emanating from Ilya, as if he was steaming. 'Well, good morning to you, you've overslept the time you should have been on duty!'

'I'm not a dog, to be on duty!' bristled the captain. 'Whatever I want to do, I will do, and don't you try to point the finger.'

'That's true,' agreed Ilya, who had a store of patience like a camel, but the captain turned away and huddled closer to the wall.

Later, feeling hungry, he forced himself to move. Over the previous few days he had forgotten about food, but now he felt an increasingly unbearable hunger, as though his food had been hidden on the other side of the wall and he could hear other people gobbling it down. 'Give me something to eat!' he suddenly demanded, with such a harsh decisiveness that Ilya was brought to his senses. It seemed to Ilya that, since turning to face the wall, the captain had been waiting far too long for his food, which they had forgotten to bring him.

They quickly laid a table for him in the office. They chucked in some gruel and a concoction made from dried fruit for him to drink. There was lots of rye bread and ruddy pieces of crackling with salt and pepper – they had used up a chunk of beef fat especially for the captain. Swallowing all this food down, Khabarov expanded and grew heavier, but still did not feel full, which is to say, happy. 'They sold us out!' he said to Ilya, flushing a livid red. 'This regiment needs to be burnt down, as an infection hazard. There's not one man in it worth taking pity on. There's sickness all around. The general rang me, but they'd sell out even a general, I know it! But I'll manage it. Look, he's on his way, which means I'll tell him what needs to be done with this regiment. Which means douse it in petrol and set it alight. Let him give me the order. Oh, I'd do it all!'

'That's right, Vania . . . ' agreed Peregud, turning sombre, and the captain spluttered, sinking into stinking oblivion. Forgetting everything he had been saying, he suddenly flushed that livid colour again, ending up like an inflated bladder. 'But they sold me out! Where can I get hold of some petrol, to burn this infection out . . . The general rang me. He's an honest man, I trust him. But they'll sell him out, they'll sell him out.'

Ilya was fed up with the captain's bilious speeches. No longer able to endure this torment, he could not hold back: 'But what can you do about it?'

'I can do everything!' exclaimed the captain. This drove Ilya beyond endurance. Recoiling from the captain, he sprang up and muttered helplessly, 'I'm not going to stay with you, you can sit here by yourself, seeing as you've become a right bastard.' The captain looked at him in surprise, his gaze ascending to the summit of that mountain, the head, and, barely restraining his anger, he said, 'That will be the death of you, Ilyushka . . . You're a parasite and a freeloader, not a Cossack. Get out of my unit.' The other man glowered and shrank into himself; turning clumsily in the narrow office and catching himself on a stool that screeched along the floor, he made his way slowly to the door, barely managing the act of walking, as though his legs were beams of wood.

Khabarov appeared before the soldiers in the cookhouse, his greed still unassuaged, despite having already put away his fourth portion. He normally joined the company for meals, sitting among the soldiers and waiting for the cauldrons to be brought out, receiving his portion in turn. For this reason the company commander was greeted as usual and many men did not even notice him as they took their seats or fought over a place. A pair of soldiers dragged in the pot, an enormous cauldron inside which an intrepid individual could have curled up like a fancy loaf of bread. It gave off a nourishing heat. The slop smelt of buns, although it might prove quite inedible, as though they had been boiling up rags in the cauldron. In their impatience, the men produced a living, human wail, every man desperate to try the slop and get some relief. It was at that instant, perhaps the most straightforward in their lives, that Khabarov sprang out, scaring them all. 'I'm about to make you very happy, you sons of bitches!' he exclaimed. 'In the name of truth and justice, I am passing sentence upon you!' He was struggling to speak, now, because he had pulled out the table along which the hot and steaming pan had been sailing, and overturned it. The cauldron toppled heavily, like a head lopped from a torso, spraying out the slop like lifeblood, drenching everything. The soldiers fought to get out of the way. Suddenly drained of strength, as though betrayed, the captain stupidly said, 'What's up, have you done eating?' No one dared answer him; mind you, no one had yet managed to gather their wits. As he left, he threatened them joylessly, 'Wait for me, now, I'll be back for dinnertime.'

With the sudden lull, the very air in the barracks turned crackly and icy, fettering not breath, but spirit. You couldn't exactly have said that the captain had been plotting, hidden away in his office, but he appeared before dinner and walked off, away from the barracks, on some matter of his own. Blindly crossing the square, the captain nonetheless halted at the shack. This was the one place in the entire company that remained dear to him; he looked it over with feeling, and he remembered. There had been no lock on the shack ever since the Special-Department agent had broken in, but even in its dilapidated state it was still imbued with that same air of activity, as if its missing resident had re-established himself within. So it came as a great surprise to Khabarov when he observed that there truly was someone living in the shack. There, where his potatoes used to be, Petr Korneichuk, the soldier who had been pulled out of the shit, was hiding from the other men. The captain barely recognised him: he was puffed up and wearing pitiful, cast-off rags. Seeing the captain, the soldier flung himself down at his feet, moved to tears of joy, and blurted out, 'Comrade Captain, you'll be amazed: the lads aren't giving me anything to eat; they've nicked my boots; they beat me up; they want me to sleep in the shithouse and not pass infection on to people . . . You'll be amazed! Amazed, I tell you, comrade Captain!'

It must have been the final straw. Khabarov fearsomely exclaimed, 'You can go to hell, the lot of you!' and ran out of the shack in a frenzy. From the sentry towers, they saw him stray off into the steppe. From time to time he would disappear from view, only to reappear, visible in the distance, standing stock-still.

When he returned to the company, Khabarov once more locked himself in the office, while his appearance before the soldiers at dinnertime, which they were expecting, almost ready to tie him up and throw him behind bars, did not come to pass after all. Having eaten without pleasure, the soldiers piled off to sleep.

In the middle of the night, a dreadful thunder and clatter was heard in the square. The men rushed quickly out of the barracks, but they saw nothing other than the shack, reduced to splinters, under whose ruins they began searching for Korneichuk. He wasn't able to speak, but he was belching; his hideously swollen belly was poking out and there was a noose around his bull neck. That night, Korneichuk had eaten the company supplies: all the beef fat, everything that was edible. In his hunger, he had eaten away the winter, he had eaten through January and February, knowing all the same that he was going to hang himself, that he would make up for it by his death.

However, the joists of the clapboard shack had not borne his weight. As a hanged man, saved by his own insides, continuing to live against his will, this was how he was found by the soldiers. They beat him up. But fearing they might beat him to death, they called for Khabarov, thinking that the captain would take the little darling away and, maybe, kill him. Khabarov led Petr Korneichuk into the steppe. The stirred-up soldiers saw them come to a halt out on the steppe, and stand there for a bit. But then Khabarov walked back to the company, while Petr Korneichuk went in the direction of the Dolinka camp, to which the captain himself had shown the way, not knowing a better alternative destination on the planet. Ivan Yakovlevich returned, looking as though he had indeed killed someone, so they feared to approach him and complain that there were no supplies left in the company. He went into the barracks averting his eyes, while the servicemen remained on the square, afraid to follow him in. But, waiting there, they heard a fusillade. Gunshots shook the barracks for a long time, just like a piledriver at work. When it all went quiet, they still did not go in for a long time. The first to look into the office saw that Khabarov was still alive. The air was smoky from burning gunpowder, but the captain himself was lying, eyes open, on the bunk, completely covered in snowy lime that had flaked off the ceiling, in which bullet holes shone like stars: he had emptied a full clip into the empty ceiling.

•

From that day, from the moment of that fusillade, Khabarov refused all food and drink. Throwing out his cotton-filled mattress, he lay flat on the strong metal springs, without either air or light from the heavens. Very soon the captain began to really stink, his beard grew out and he became delirious, plunging ever deeper into a mindless void. Figuring out that this wasn't a binge, that the company commander had got it into his head to exit this life, the soldiers began force-feeding him. They rolled up their sleeves, so as not to get them dirty. Then they would force open the captain's mouth with their grubby little hands and pour down all kinds of liquid swill. The feeders appeared to him as regimental quartermasters intending to evict him, and the captain would groan, 'Wait, leave me alone . . . I'm dying, see . . . '

But there was no one left to look after the captain, because Ilya Peregud had not returned to the company. On the day that Khabarov drove him out, he had decided to leave for Ugolpunkt for good. He got on the narrow-gauge railway, with the prison warders, and off he went. These men, his dear old friends, began to vituperate Khabarov, for whom Ilya had deserted them in years past. Ilya listened to them and began swearing about the captain himself, but suddenly he grew angry and set about defending the captain, so hotly that he threw anyone who spoke poorly of Khabarov from the train, and at Stepnoi he tore up a section of track, putting an end to traffic along the whole branch line. By the time he made it to Ugolpunkt, where the maimed prison warders had put in complaints about him, they came to escort him to the guardhouse over this misdemeanour. He likewise shrugged off his escort, and nearly brought the living quarters down around their ears; had the battalion commander not managed to placate him by promising not to shave his head and to allow him to consume vodka in the guardhouse, there might have been havoc wrought all over town.

At these most cheerless of times, a regimental lorry arrived in Karabas, laden to the brim with potatoes, only they were rotten. Their foul smell seeped out from the back of the truck. The soldiers driving it said that they were bringing back the very same potatoes that had been taken from the company in the autumn. Just as many sacks as were shown on the inventory. They also brought news that there had been a change of command at the regiment. They informed the company about their old colonel: he was no longer at the regiment; apparently some general had arrived and imposed order.

A day or so later, they celebrated New Year in the company, grubbing together a celebratory meal from the rotten potatoes. The captain was rotting alive in the grave of his office, unaware that a new era was dawning. They tried to share some of the potatoes with him. They rammed potatoes into his mouth, willing him to chew, but he spat them out.

8

A NEW ERA

As if part of his brain had been eaten away, Petr Vale-rianovich Degtiar knew no fear, unless you count an enduring embarrassment over his bald spot, which was threatening from above to turn him into a laughing stock. Deputising for Pobedov during his illness, Degtiar had had time to get used to this new position, restoring order to the singed regimental affairs, hurrying to put everything right before the inspection. He never once visited Fyodor Fyodorovich in the hospital, and only when it became known that the regimental commander was about to be discharged in good health did he plan to go – with a heavy heart, as if having to visit a man who was dying.

The management had set the hospital up with such a sheen that it looked like a spa. It was surrounded by a well-tended park, with avenues and benches; on its surface swam the hospital, looking like a cruise ship. In it, meritorious people – that is, war veterans and senior officers from the region – restored their health. Pobedov had already been transferred to a convalescent ward, impinging on a retired general there. This general considered himself in charge of the ward. The general wore his towelling dressing gown nonchalantly, as if done up to the nines in a felt cloak from the Caucasus. His uniform, even in the hospital, consisted of a crisp shirt and trousers with red stripes running down the side. He wandered about the ward with the handset from a radio receiver of the best workmanship, from which news incessantly churned out: from building projects to factories and fields . . . He would listen to them, his hard head slightly slanted, as if he'd put his neck out, and now and then would set matters straight: 'Now that's right, that's right, that I approve . . . Well, what are they looking at, I would give them all a good thrashing! Ah, but that's good, that's good.' This thing, this receiver, was valuable in and of itself, but everything pointed to the fact that the general had received it as an award, maybe for long service, which was why he valued it and would not let his award slip from his grasp. Degtiar and the colonel had to withdraw so as not to alarm him.

Pobedov looked tired. He was afraid of being the first to ask what was happening in the regiment, although he had found everything out second-hand from other people. 'How's your health?' asked Petr Valerianovich. The colonel hastened to fall ill again. 'I can't breathe, I have these bouts. If I could just make it through this inspection . . . They've ruined my regiment for me, the shitheads, but just watch, they'll be sent flying once I get back . . . ' Degtiar then set about guiltily reporting what he had been doing and how he had been doing it in the colonel's absence. Pobedov listened to him with a cold, contented air; he was enjoying the fact that the adjutant had presented himself after all, and was patiently hearing out the colonel's reproaches; that is, he wasn't protesting. Gaining vigour, the colonel even took pleasure in giving the adjutant a rather crude dressing-down: 'Take your bloody hat off, man, you're indoors.' Hurt, Degtiar removed his headgear. Pobedov cut him off once again: 'So, I bet you've been trying my office out for size? Hang on a bit, I'll be sitting there a little longer myself. Support me a little, then we'll see.'

Degtiar could not restrain himself. 'Fyodor Fyodorovich, I don't understand, I've always followed orders.'

'Followed orders, he says . . . But try waiting for some gratitude from you,' complained the colonel, in a weaker voice. 'You might at least have got a parcel together, shown some consideration. Other people get them brought, but I've nothing in my bedside cabinet. It's embarrassing, really.' Degtiar stood. 'Where are you off to?' frowned Fyodor Fyodorovich.

'I'm going back to the base.'

'Off you go, then, off you go . . . I'm told you left Skripitsyn in place? Well, all right. Give that saboteur my regards. I'll have another talk with him, maybe I'll forgive him.' He rose, with a groan. His government-issue dressing gown was too big for him, although its stitching and cut were impeccable. Turning away, he stumbled back to his ward and knocked. 'Comrade Lieutenant-General, permission to enter?'

November in Karaganda in some way resembled the white nights of the north. The town air was cool, clear and fresh. That was the month when neither snow nor rain fell. The earth dried out, like laundry in a frost. It got cold in the evenings, as though winter had come into the town to stay, but as soon as day began to break, it warmed up all around and winter left.

Discharged from the hospital, Fyodor Fyodorovich hurried back to the regiment, where they had somehow already managed to restore order after the ruinous fire. Degtiar once more stepped to the side as the colonel returned; it seemed he hadn't so much moved aside as buried himself underground. Pobedov decided for now to pay no heed to Skripitsyn, who had been relieved of his post but allowed to remain in the regiment. He roamed around like a lone horse. No one knew which general would appear to conduct the inspection but, during those days, each man in the know recounted hotly that this general could not be bought off at any price and that he seemed to be performing his duties reliant on mysterious sources of strength. The Asiatic districts were inspected, including the regiments in Tashkent, Ashkhabad and Frunze, from which came the most chilling rumours about a General Dobychin, a new man, merciless, the likes of which the army had never seen before. However, nothing changed as a result of these rumours and it was the same old Karaganda, nestling under drowsy rays of sunlight just before the winter, that greeted General Dobychin.

When they finally saw the actual Dobychin, the regiment experienced yet another shock: out of the car climbed a tall Tatar; not elderly at all, but rather in the very prime of life; handsome like silver, and not darkened by spite. Perhaps he wasn't even a Tatar; whatever his ethnic background, though, his character dazzled with inspiration. Strength was imprinted all over his appearance. His eyes were narrow, his cheekbones high, his mouth held tightly shut; he was sinewy and tough. He stood out from the people surrounding him, although the general was accompanied by small men who would have appeared sycophantic no matter what pose they adopted. And this created a surprising sight: it was as if a wolf were chasing a herd of sheep yet was not at all hungry; he had no desire to devour them. They, meanwhile, were servile, as if they had grown hungry and were asking for something to eat. And so, while there was nothing ghastly about Dobychin's appearance, he still seemed frightening, even merciless. However, when he saw that the regiment's commander was elderly, Dobychin treated the colonel with great respect; that is, he shook him personally by the hand, which nearly led Fyodor Fyodorovich's arm to drop off, because such a thing had never happened to him in all his years of service.

So it became known that Dobychin had respect for old men after all, and that he was a true general, who would decide everything himself, on the spot.

The regiment had assembled on the square for his arrival. They took pride in their parades and their band was carefully chosen. The bandmaster himself travelled around as a recruiting officer, searching out French horn players and trumpeters among the hordes of people who had been sent off for military service. He was capable of giving up two strapping Ukrainian lads, brought up on a healthy diet of dumplings and sour cream, to another recruiter in exchange for a sickly Jewish boy who had known the whole truth about the bass clef since childhood. A parade like this would dazzle any general lucky enough to inspect it – so much blood must have been expended on the distillation of cast-iron marches out of living souls whipped into endless ranks.

Pobedov had unexpectedly regained some of his youth and, as he commanded the sections on parade, his voice rang out around the square. His arms and legs began to resound like ripe watermelons when he suddenly sprang across to the general to offer his salute. And when he had saluted, he did not stand behind the general, as the other lower-ranking regimental officers were doing, but showed the general his back, doing an 'abo-o-out, turn' and, thrusting his leg out like a bayonet, marched towards the regiment, which was drawn up at a standstill, where he stood under the colours, in their shade. And it was he who shouted, 'Forward, ma-a-a-rch!', stretching out his voice like a bugle call. Many could not hide their alarm, scared that the colonel would knock them all out of step, causing the hitherto serried ranks to fold up like a concertina, but Fyodor Fyodorovich socked it to them so hard that, gasping for breath, the whole regiment set off joyfully behind him, their very own dashing commander. Dobychin patiently watched the whole parade, but remained unmoved. 'You know how to walk, then . . . ' he said, dryly and without warmth, to the colonel who had skipped up to receive his praise, all in a lather. And so another discovery was made: that Dobychin was far from being soldierly by nature since he did not understand and appreciate the beauty of the drill.

With far greater goodwill, the general took a stroll around the base. He looked into everything, interested by all that he saw. However, a certain glint, albeit tarnished, had crept into his eye. This indicated more clearly that there was nothing for him to do there, as if he had flown in from another world. It must have been a drag for Dobychin to inspect units like these, where he wasted his time for nothing, taking part in contemptible charades arranged on the occasion of his arrival.

He turned to the colonel and said, part jesting but also with menace (although the latter out of boredom), 'You had a fire here recently.'

'Yes sir, comrade General, this fact did take place,' mumbled the colonel. 'Things burned.'

'Fresh air, was it, that burned?' Dobychin had grown tired of waiting for a straight answer.

'No sir, it was the lorry park,' replied Pobedov, great drops of sweat breaking out and pouring, not even like paint, but like his own vivid crimson blood, since the general had stopped right by the lorry park itself. The charred concrete had been scraped away and gnawed at, like a bone. The hangars had been rebuilt, and for a bit of prettiness they had stuck a few trees in the ground. 'So what was it that burned here?' exclaimed Dobychin, provoked into anger after all. His exclamation hung in the air, then was suddenly caught up by a sack-like figure holding a briefcase who had been hiding in the shadows behind other people's backs, but who now began to make his way through the crowd, to widespread alarm.

'Comrade General! It was the truth that burned here, comrade General!'

Skripitsyn had jumped in and begun swimming through the heads, hitching up his case as if he feared getting the contents wet when a ring of these liquid people caught hold of his shoulders, trying to sink him, but not even a tempest at sea could have stopped this desperate man; he emerged at the general's feet with such a sorry look, it was as if he truly had spent some time under water. 'Who on earth is this?' asked Dobychin, not in fright but surprise.

'This man used to be the head of my Special Department. We even wanted to court-martial him, comrade General . . . ' Fyodor Fyodorovich hurriedly spoke up, dazed by fear; it seemed to him that his very life was ending. And it wasn't clear what the general intended when he unhesitatingly gave an order to his officers, who had seized hold of the trembling Skripitsyn: 'Bring this seeker of truth to me afterwards . . . '

'Comrade General –' Pobedov tried to explain, but Dobychin had once more turned morose.

When they slowly moved away from that spot, it seemed that the regiment was not being inspected but buried; almost as though in front of them a coffin was being borne along on pall-bearers' shoulders. Their faces could not have been more mournful and the colonel was clutching at his chest, although Dobychin had begun talking calmly to him, as if seeking explanation for something he had seen. When he found out as they were walking that the old colonel had deliberately discharged himself from the hospital, he even clapped Fyodor Fyodorovich on the shoulder. 'Well, what did you do that for? You should have made sure you were better . . . '

'Yes sir, yes sir.' The colonel was touched. They had laid tables in the HQ canteen and the general was invited to dine richly, but they all ate as though conducting a wake. This dinner brought the first day of Dobychin's visit to an end. The next day he was due to hold a Party meeting in the regiment, in order to convey the Party's current policies.

Towards midday, when the meeting was scheduled to start, servicemen began arriving at the regimental base from all its companies. These were battalion commanders, as well as those chosen from among the Party members, men who had already been around the block once or twice. The trip out was a holiday for these men: here they met their old comrades, their muckers, who had been scattered about by the demands of the service. They piled into the clubhouse as if it was someone's home, for some reason wiping their feet as they went in. The ones who managed to find a seat flung their arms out to embrace their comrades, like dear guests, for whom they had kept the neighbouring seats free in readiness. Their happy buzz quietened when the members of the presidium took their places behind three tables covered with red calico on the podium. This podium wasn't high; it was more like a tall step. Everyone sought out the general. Shining foreheads paved the stilled clubhouse, and the speeches began marching out as though along a living parade square.

General Dobychin opened the meeting with his report, expressing himself so clearly it was as if he was cutting out just the words he wanted in swathes from the fresh air before their very eyes. Next, Pobedov gave his report. The way some people remembered it afterwards, his speech was forceful, as usual; although others, no fewer in number, maintained that as the colonel stood at the rostrum he was swaying and could hardly move his tongue.

The air in the clubhouse grew stuffy. 'Comrade Andropov blah-blah-blah Yurii Vladimirovich blah-blah-blah the general secretary blah-blah-blah the Party.' Such words paced along the foreheads, dying off somewhere towards the back rows. When Dobychin clapped, the room was filled with clapping, as though by order. At the end, the voting took place. The servicemen could not remember what had been discussed in any detail and they voted in a forest of arms, generally relieved and glad to support all the Party's decisions. When Colonel Pobedov declared the meeting closed, the clubhouse filled with a heavy buzz.

'So what's the story with this captain you had who planted potatoes?' asked Dobychin suddenly, and mockingly, as they headed for the exit. Pobedov stood at attention and let fall the words, 'No sir, comrade General, we put a stop to that madness, have no doubt.' The general grew downcast; his handsome face darkened. It was clear that the old colonel's answer had depressed him; it wasn't what he had been looking for.

'Back when I was still on front-line duties, a report came, also from an army base, that they had caught a spy. The Special Department had done its job,' Dobychin began talking with complete seriousness. 'When I get there, a young soldier is sitting in the cells; the milk hasn't dried on his lips. I say, "What sort of spy do you call him?" They produce a tattered book in a foreign language. "Look," they say, "he reads this at night and makes notes." And do you know what kind of book it turned out to be? It was a textbook for students of English! It's as well I at least managed to get the lad out of there. Maybe a clever head will manage to clamber out of this thistle patch of ours, and he'll even know foreign languages.'

'Yes! Yes!' rang out all round, each man trying to be louder than the rest. Dobychin had calmed down when, suddenly, a man emerged from behind the colonel, where he had gone unnoticed all this time, which is not to imply he might have been *worth* ignoring . . .

It was the adjutant, Degtiar. In a sort of daze, he hurried to report through the hush that had descended: 'But here in the regiment, comrade General, these clever heads are dying off; we had seven soldiers . . . ' But Dobychin, almost in disgust, cut him off: 'You idiot.' Then he sought out Pobedov with his eyes and barked, 'And so are you. It's way past time for you to retire, hand your cards in.'

'Yes sir, comrade General . . . ' babbled Fyodor Fyodorovich, leaning way back just as though the general was breathing fire at him. 'They hang on until you have to court-martial them . . . ' growled Dobychin.

The servicemen still crowding by the doorway were surprised to hear this from the general. They stepped back respectfully, making way for Dobychin. He looked around and caught a last distant glimpse of the old man, writhing on the empty podium. He had slumped over onto the presidium table as though he was choking; he was clutching his chest. Dobychin could not resist a condescending barb: 'The old guard dies . . . It dies, and it dies . . . '

They heard him and so they poured after him, fearing to remain in the clubhouse. Shoved completely out of the way, Degtiar brought up the very rear, gasping desperately for air and not understanding anything going on around him. 'Comrades, help me . . . ' He heard the colonel's call, but was too scared to turn round.

They all left. The club was deserted. Bereft of strength, Pobedov's torso collapsed onto the red calico-covered presidium table, and he began to wheeze.

No one caught hold of the old man, everyone fled; none of them could wait to get the hell out of that meeting. The soldiers, meanwhile, couldn't be bothered clearing up the clubhouse that same evening and instead quietly turned up the next morning to do some lackadaisical tidying. Overnight, the hungry clubhouse rats had gnawed at the dead colonel's legs, chewing off his genuine cowhide officer's boots, of which there remained bits of stony sole and hobnails under the presidium table.

It was said that when he heard of this death, General Dobychin burst into tears. Setting himself up temporarily in the old colonel's office, he summoned the adjutant Petr Valerianovich Degtiar. 'This means that you'll take command of this here regiment for me, as you wanted,' he said. He had expected to find Degtiar an example of the lowest of mankind, but instead discovering a featureless stump of a man, like an iron nail, he said no more, dismissing him with those words. Then, mulling things over, he remembered that he had ordered the man who had started it all to be brought to him. Skripitsyn was sought out and brought in; they led him into the office looking like a man sentenced to face the firing squad: made stupid, with a kind of fishy, cold gravity escaping into his vacant, wide-open eyes. Struggling to master his wrath, Dobychin muttered, 'So that's what kind of man you are . . . Are you scared, now? Have you got a mother and father?'

'They are not around . . . ' said the other man, with unwilling obsequiousness, and promptly shut up.

'Did you have no pity for that old man, who could have been your father?' Their eyes met. Skripitsyn was staring, no longer able to conceal his amazement. 'I was telling the truth about the comrade colonel . . . They criticised him, and he died.' And the general leapt up from behind the desk, shouting, 'You rotten bastard!'

Looking as if they were done up in lacquered tunics, the black cars soon drove away from the lifeless regiment. Back at HQ, where the cars pulled up, as Dobychin got out and made for the doorway, he could not get that surname out of his mind. 'Skripitsyn, Skripitsyn . . . Should I reinstate him, then? What post did he hold there, anyway?' He flung this out morosely as he went, and those nearby only happened to hear him.

The light in the old colonel's office window was out. Maybe General Dobychin himself had extinguished it as he was leaving. The regiment descended into a deathly gloom. Compelled to stand vigilantly at their posts, the sentries spent that night in dejection. They looked out into the steely darkness, in which they were scarcely able to discern the dim outlines of the base, and quivered at every sound behind them, which never used to happen before. It used to be that you'd be stamping your feet, frozen through and hungry, but far off the colonel's window would be blazing for everyone, like you could light up a cig from it. And even if they all knew that there was no one in the office, it still made them all calmer thanks to this gift of a flare, left on view by the old man to steady their nerves. The sentries that night could not comprehend that the light had gone out for good. They complained that the dark had been let in; that the bosses did not stint on light for themselves, but rationed it out to the men. They also could not comprehend what purpose the inspection had served. The general had been and gone. He'd made just the one appointment, but what an appointment that had been. He had removed one colonel, but what a removal that had been. Where he'd found the time to look was where it had all happened, and that had been the entire inspection, even though it seemed like they had been waiting a whole year to find out who would attract a brief comment or who would catch his eye. However, the reputation that followed General Dobychin, that he was a man without mercy, took even stronger root. This being the year they recognised his character, in the army they even gave him the nickname Batu Khan.

When Petr Valerianovich Degtiar turned up for work at the regiment, the duty officer did not report to him or even salute him, despite the other soldiers watching. They looked askance at him from all sides and whispered. Only in the anteroom did Senior Lieutenant Sokolskii break into a smile. 'Good morning to you, comrade Lieutenant Colonel, my congratulations . . . ' Degtiar averted his eyes guiltily and went through into the office. He looked out of the window in torment. A soldier was stirring up clouds of dust on the parade square with a broom that haphazardly sprouted bristles. From a lorry that had pulled up next to the cookhouse, soldiers were unloading freshly baked bread. Life went on its way, as per routine, yet Degtiar could no longer go out onto the square and simply strike up a conversation with these soldiers, to whom he had become alien. And everyone else was holding out to see who would be brave enough to speak to Degtiar first.

The first to appear in the regimental commander's office was Skripitsyn. He went in without knocking, as was his wont, slamming the door as strongly as he could, right in Sokolskii's face. 'I've come to tell you that I respect you; you haven't changed in my eyes. I know how to remember a good turn, Petr Valerianovich,' Skripitsyn deigned to say. 'We're all human, everyone makes mistakes in life. But I don't blame you for the colonel's death. We'll bury him with full honours, no matter what happened, and he deserved full honours, what with being commander for so long. In fact I came to talk about the burial. It wouldn't do to put the matter off . . . ' Not knowing he was doing it, or, more likely, knowing it only too well, Skripitsyn lifted the heaviest burden from the lieutenant colonel. Degtiar felt ashamed that Skripitsyn had been merciful, as though he had offered a transfusion of his own blood and Degtiar had been ashamed to take it. They talked it all through; that is, Petr Valerianovich agreed with relief to the entire procedure that Skripitsyn was suggesting. Not to bring the body onto the base, but to lay it out in the Karaganda Officers' Club, posting just an honour guard around the coffin, and then on to the cemetery, the military one, where a salvo in the colonel's honour was to be permitted. That was all there would be to it. 'There's a certain other matter, I don't know how this will go down . . . ' said Skripitsyn. 'The colonel occupied some living space, a single room. You couldn't make a museum out of it, and he doesn't seem to have left any descendants. Meanwhile, I've spent seven years living in hostels. All the HQ men here have set themselves up all right, with their wives. Could you not turn that living space over to me? How do you see it, Petr Valerianovich? It's an indelicate question, but best not put it off . . . '

'I've no objections, Anatolii,' replied Degtiar, unthinkingly. When Skripitsyn had left, Sokolskii ran into the office. 'Comrade Lieutenant Colonel, I'm an officer, I demand that I be provided with accommodation. You're giving that flat to the man who stained it with blood. But I loved Fyodor Fyodorovich.' At that instant, Degtiar regained his prior strength of will, driving himself back into it like a nail. 'He killed for the flat, you loved for the flat, while I loved and killed . . . ' But his will just then gave out and, listlessly, embarrassed, he said, 'Anatolii has been in the regiment longer than you, he needs it.'

Whether or not it was Senior Lieutenant Sokolskii who started the rumour, from that day on they began saying in the regiment that Skripitsyn was in charge of everything and that Degtiar had acceded to this with relief. The general's words protected Skripitsyn better than any armour. Even at divisional HQ they knew who had noticed the Special-Department head.

It was at this time that Skripitsyn devised the notion of sending a consignment of potatoes off to Sixth Company, as though to return what he had taken away.

He even thought of Captain Khabarov with pleasure now, for some reason. 'Make sure they pass on my best wishes to Ivan Yakovlevich!' No matter how much Skripitsyn fancied showing off, though, he didn't follow anything up, and so, as per usual, they sent off nothing but rotten stuff.

He celebrated New Year with a flutter in his soul, sensing the beginning of a new era that would somehow be very important for him. However, once the festivities were over, he grew cautious, expecting that captain from the steppes to show up in gratitude any day now, although he never did.

Once he'd begun trying to find things out, to sniff around, Skripitsyn noticed that the forgotten settlement had by now been silent for a long time; that the regimental duty officers were themselves having to extract bulletins from the distant company, and they had already managed to report to HQ that there didn't seem to be anyone in charge at the Sixth. Skripitsyn called the company on the direct line and spoke to God knows who, so he was hardly able to extract any firm facts. 'What about the captain?'

'He's-a here, he's-a dying, everyone's-a dying here, they found some dead potatoes round here. They brought some more in, rotten, they all got scoffed. There's no one in charge, the captain's gone off to die. There's-a not enough eats here, all the eats have gone missing somewhere.'

Skripitsyn took himself off on a mission the next day, not making a big noise about it on the base. Afraid to go, he was also afraid of putting it off, and so you couldn't say what force it was that lifted him from his seat and moved him to Karabas.

The lorry came to rest on the lifeless, deserted barrack square. As though they had been unloading sacks of flour, the square was lightly dusted in snow. Winter had yet to set in just there, or in the whole steppe, for that matter. Spreading snow across the yard, imprinting powdery white tracks with his boots, the Special-Department agent went into the barracks, where the emptiness, like a hungry mouth, exhaled a vapour that made your head spin. Maybe because his head had started spinning and he had suddenly lost his ever fragile willpower, Skripitsyn ran first for the administrative office, finding there the man he sought.

The office was enormous, and terrifying: the walls there had wasted away, so that the oily paint had burst apart; the floor had given way and the ceiling had fallen in. Everything within was dead and withered; objects looked either like dried fish or greying paper. Khabarov was lying, completely uncovered, in some kind of woman's woollen sweater, with no underwear whatsoever. Everything that had come out of him was heaped in a soiled vessel under the bunk. At the sight of this hopelessly ragged sweater, out of which a moss-covered log was seemingly poking, Skripitsyn was all set to flee, deciding to have nothing to do with a corpse, but a creak came from the log, and there was movement.

Skripitsyn began to wail, to call out for someone, anyone, to help. At his order they dragged the bunk with the dying captain on it out into the chilly corridor. Once they had dragged the captain out, they made as if to disperse, but Skripitsyn had the presence of mind to say, 'Cover him up with something, at least. Something good and warm . . . ' He himself set out, at first unsteady and shaking, but with each step more and more angry and determined, to find the remaining men. He wanted to gather them together and punish every last man who was there.

There were men in the barracks, but it seemed their numbers had diminished. Recognising Skripitsyn, the soldiers had vanished as if the very ground had swallowed them up. It took Skripitsyn a long time to gather the men and bring them to their senses enough that they would set about carrying out his orders, by which time he had already managed to gradually to lose his anger.

He sat day and night at Khabarov's bunk, afraid to leave him alone, although the captain's resolve had broken and he was slowly putting on weight before the special agent's eyes. Skripitsyn did not take the captain to hospital, as he could have, but waited in torment for the other man to come round. It happened that, lying in clean underwear, in the warmth, and scrubbed to a waxy shine, the captain took a look at the world and his eyes filled with tears in surprise. Instantly tiring, they closed and dried up, like soil, but all the same a small ray of light made its way out of them in the other direction. One morning, as he was languishing away during this extended mission, Skripitsyn finally achieved his aim: looking around with clarity, the captain started speaking to him.

He had been unswaddled, his hands lay on a rough wool bedspread, warming themselves as they never had before, pressing the palms together. He was breathing evenly and cleanly, at which Skripitsyn himself felt his spirits lift. 'Don't worry, father, I haven't come to arrest you,' he said in a single outburst, scared of frightening the captain. But Khabarov looked at him with that same clarity, and found his voice. 'I'm not worried, though.' The Special-Department agent hesitated, with an unpleasant sense of surprise, but he could not bring himself to begin, so he set about complaining, with a barely audible reproach. 'You're a proud man, but I am not. You're proud, but me . . . This is what your pride is like: what's good for me is instantly bad for you. So what am I to do with you?' He looked hungrily at the captain, demanding a reply, and for his sake Khabarov forced himself to speak again, although his voice still sounded simple and ordinary: 'Forgive me for everything, if you can.' Skripitsyn was dumbfounded, helplessly gulping air, which lasted for an instant while he became aware of something, and then

he took on a grand, albeit trembling, air. 'But will you forgive me?' Unable to contain himself, he slumped, hiding
his face behind his ugly hands, and he started to mutter
through the gaps. 'I'm in charge now at the regiment, so
you know this: we'll do just what you want. You'll have
everything! Haven't you got a house? Well, I'll build you
a whole town here, and you'll be in charge. I'll have trees
flourishing here, watermelon trees! Everything, father.
Make use of it, you've made it this far . . . '

'I have forgiven you, now you forgive me . . . '
repeated Khabarov. But Skripitsyn was not listening to
him, carried away by his new goal. 'So just wait for spring,
you just wait, and you'll have everything!'

When he found out that Skripitsyn had driven off,
the captain got up and gradually began to try and walk.
Somehow he made it out onto the square, still weak, but
with a haversack over his shoulders, and the men began
to gather of their own accord around him, hoping to
understand what was going on. 'I'm heading off, lads . . .
Farewell . . . ' breathed Khabarov. 'You'll have another
commander, that's all right. All I want to do is die with
my conscience clear. I'll wander around and look for a
place where I won't bring misfortune down on people.'
With these words he set out on his way, but he had barely
left the settlement when they grew sorry to let him go
and so ran after him, complaining when they caught up
that it was difficult to eat the rotten stuff from the regiment along with the stuff that had gone off, and they
also started asking for advice as to how they should do

their duties and what they might live on. The captain dragged his feet, sighed, and turned back for the company, so as to take a proper leave of the place and its people, which he had begun to regret not doing. During that day he talked himself into staying on for another day, so that his health grew stronger, which meant that he was lumbered with still more to do. And so he decided to stay and see the winter out in Karabas, and come the spring he would set out with a clear conscience to find a place on the earth where he could die if he wanted to. So it was that his service arranged itself into the quietest possible routine. Although Khabarov had shouldered his earlier burdens and not his light haversack, the men in the settlement paid him no heed, and he too kept away from people, and maybe even hid. When they came to him seeking orders, Khabarov was certain of nothing, scared of making mistakes, so they went away again: they could decide for themselves without hesitation and more quickly. And they said of him, 'Look what a good commander the captain has turned out to be, so soft you could spread him on bread.'

'This is why he's kind: he's quietened down, what with the hard time he's had.'

9

A FEAT IN WINTER

Khabarov loved a quiet, frozen winter: things were fine, then, both outside and within your soul. In such a winter, the huts on the Russian flatlands are wreathed in stove smoke, just like incense. The villages on those huge expanses stand covered in hoarfrost and immersed in the tall silence of the heavens. Even the dogs scattered about the yards do not bark, and a Christian peace slumbers in the thick snow. If nothing else, place a candle before this picture, far more wondrous than any holy image . . . Our ill-starred captain remembered this quiet, frozen winter from his childhood; perhaps he hadn't ever seen anything else that was good.

The winters in Karabas could be mean. They brought blizzards, and although one of those days from the captain's childhood would occasionally happen, bringing that ruddy tinge to the cheeks, the blizzards would always sweep in again, the cold would grow ferocious and the short days would be obscured by a blueish haze. But recently, in the last couple of years, the winters had been all messed up. Rumour had it that nature had slipped out of joint on a global scale, so there was nothing for it now but to await disaster. Sometimes snow would fall or rain would suddenly sheet down in December, so that the earth was encased in dirty blocks of ice. In short, the disorder stretched as far as the very heavens.

In the new year, winter did not start until February; it had overslept. And, quick to enact reprisals, it buried Karabas in deep snow, freezing everything, even the coal stored in the bunkers. They had to hew it out with crowbars. It melted, but it didn't burn. Even the lightbulbs in the rooms were covered in frost, and quietly popped. The camp was saved by its searchlights, while they burned paraffin lamps in the barracks and the guardhouse.

The servicemen worked even harder to make it through this miserable time, even if it seemed that the next day no one would be able to rouse them from their hard beds, onto which they dropped in their sheepskin coats, their felt boots and fur caps with the ear-flaps on. They were huddled together side by side, as if growing closer as the very end drew near. The men came to their senses in torment when the sentry on duty yelled reveille, tearing them from oblivion. The same man would try and light the stove, but his frigid hands would not respond, and the barracks was plunged into a miserable commotion, just like a prison. The men would fall once more back into oblivion, but the sentry would yell again, although he knew perfectly well that no one would move until the stove got going. Then every inhabitant would cluster around the grate as it blazed with heat. Receiving orders from no one, they would stare dully into the fire, endlessly shovelling coal into the gaping maw of the stove. They were still clad in the same coats and boots in which they had tumbled down to sleep, and they continued to doze, although by now they had huddled up by the stove. Their boots steamed and pillars of vapour rose up from their sheepskins, so you would have thought life itself was dissolving. When the coal scuttle, which had been positioned so as to entice people close to the fire, was empty, the order went out to fetch the rations. And off the men went, pulling themselves away from the extinguished stove, heading off for a mess tin of hot swill. Once they had gulped that down, they wouldn't stand up again. They would chew on the everlasting crusts of rye bread, waiting for someone to dollop out more swill, a bit hotter this time. Meanwhile, overnight, the barrack square would have been covered in snow. They would have just dug it out and, here you go, dig it out again. Give it another day, and more snow would fall down from the roofs. Waiting pointlessly in the cookhouse, managing in that time to get both freezing cold and starving hungry, these lads with their hearty appetites would dig out spades and toil with them in the cold and dark. Work, do your duty, and then you'll get your grub. Survive, see out this day, and then another one will dawn.

The captain had been baked from the same mortal dough as all the other men. He was a living person, all of whose power resided in the state of his health and the strength of his arms. This man had hoped his arms would always be so strong and his health so good that he'd be ashamed to worry over it, then he'd gone and overstrained himself, resulting in a hernia, as though a second stomach, a hefty little sack, had come bulging out from the first. He had also hoped that he would be able to set up a fair system, so that people might live more happily and with fuller stomachs than had so far been the case. If the captain himself could have been in charge of bread for everyone and grief for everyone, then he could have cheered and filled them up, by divvying up his own ration and opening his soul to other people's upsets. But Khabarov was not that unusual man among men after all, because as he made his way through life he, too, did not get enough to eat and grew mournful, gradually becoming just as half-starved and just as miserable as the others.

At that time there was just one thing on their minds: payday, which was coming ever nearer. The whole month's salary was due: seven roubles each. Since the sentry company did not have its own army shop, they converted their pay into goods from the camp stall. From that stall, they breathed in the head-spinning smoke of a fantasy: that they would turn up and get tobacco, butter, jam, canned meat and chocolates! A sack of money was usually flung off the train as it passed through Stepnoi without stopping, and they hardly had a chance to grab the receipt, which came with the company's couriers, in exchange. The paymaster, like the battalion HQ, was located in Ugolpunkt, where the company waited for the cherished summons to meet the train. In winter, though, the train only travelled this line every three days, and then only if there wasn't much snow. There was no other way to get to the distant company, apart from maybe a helicopter. But the rails tended to get blocked, and it might take a week to clear the snowdrifts. The narrow-gauge engine would not run at all, and for this reason the shift would be extended, so that their twenty-four-hour stints turned into weeks, or they would send a team of tractors – a home-made train – to fetch raw materials for the camp factory.

All of this was well known to the men in Sixth Company, but as no one wanted to believe their pay might be delayed, they could not bring themselves to do it. They were bitter, as if their superiors had deliberately piled snow onto the tracks in order not to pay them. Their superiors, though, were not refusing to pay, and so were not to blame, which the soldiers in Karabas did not want to understand. Payday was postponed in all the camp companies buried out in the steppe, although it may have been that the wages were handed over in Ugolpunkt itself for the fourth and fifth companies, who were closer to the battalion than the steppe settlements. For the soldiers, however, this itself justified the conclusion that they had been cheated and overlooked, and for demanding their pay regardless of snowdrifts; that is, for demanding equal treatment when, for reasons known to all, this was not to be had.

Every day in Karabas was spent trying to keep warm round the stove and to get hold of a portion of food that had just a little bit more to it, but they refused to tolerate such a life if it wasn't going to include any wages.

Agitation began among those ailing soldiers who were suffering for lack of a hospital. There were around a dozen of them: chilled, frostbitten and emaciated. An order had recently gone round the regiment that anyone who fell ill should be treated on the spot, not sent to hospital. The order had gone out because the very existence of hospital beds significantly weakened discipline. The soldiers deliberately harmed themselves, especially in winter, when it was easy to throw water over yourself and catch a chill. On the spot, though, there was now neither treatment to be had nor medicine. The ill either pulled through or fell down dead. When the poorly individuals found out about the money being delayed at the battalion, they set about whingeing quietly, 'We'll all die here . . . They've stolen our money . . . They'll give us one month's pay instead of two . . . ' No one had the strength to withstand their whining. They lay on their cots, wrapped in whatever came to hand, great mounds that looked like hills. The healthy men, too, grew sour in the darkness, surrounded by bare frosty walls. Looking at these walls was equivalent to banging your head against them. And into this void was born a furious, fearless battle cry: 'Brothers, here's what we demand: give us our pay! We're being robbed!'

While this angry brew was coming to the boil, the captain, already driven to despair, was on his way to ask the camp for cash loans for his soldiers, with his promise as bond. Apart from his promise, he had nothing else to offer.

The captain was thinking he would seek forgiveness from Sinebriukhov, who might take pity on them, but he found out that, some months ago now, the previous camp commandant had been found guilty of misappropriation on a quite spectacular scale. The new commandant, a burly fellow exuding health next to whom the captain looked like a *zek*, did not refuse straight away. He let the captain amuse him, listening to his request with pleasure, as though assessing whether or not to believe in the captain's promise. But Khabarov's requests became increasingly bitter and complaining, and the big man used his strong frame to push away this captain who was trying to put the screws on him. 'This is not some kind of privately run gangster outfit; it's a state undertaking, you moron. I have accountability. The cashier from the regional administration keeps coming to take the proceeds and everything's got to be done according to the law, even if you have to make up the difference with your gold teeth.' Maybe the new boss was hinting at something, but Khabarov did not pick up on it. When it became clear to the fellow that there was no profit to be extracted from the company captain, not even his hide, he spewed obscenities at him and almost threw a few punches in for good measure, bundling him aggressively out of the stores.

The same desolation reigned in the zone as every-where else, but banging could be heard: the workshops were still going at this hour. The sentry towers rose up like ladders into the hazy sky. The captain could make out that they were empty, standing there unmanned, as though taken by storm. At the gatehouse Khabarov ran into some warders, who were hurriedly battening down all the entrances and exits. They turned to him to ask, 'Here, what's going on? The camp has never been left unguarded before. Go and let your lads know, quickly, tell them, so that we catch the *zeks* unawares. What are you stood there saying nothing for? Get yourself out of here, or they'll burn you up with the rest.' But the cap-tain didn't hear them. Exchanging glances, the warders stepped away from him, crunching the snow under their feet and saying, 'He's done for, that bloke . . . '

'Aw, good riddance, the bastard. He's not been right for ages, that one; he's hung on, trying to take us all to the grave with him.' The guards had run off. Only a guard dog was flinging itself about and howling, abandoned on the parade square. She joyously latched on to the captain, standing close to him, and quietly tagged along behind, when he returned to the company empty-handed. But then, once he'd examined the gates, from which a dusting of snow had fallen, as though they had been breathing frost, he could no longer see the dog either beside him or anywhere about the barrack square. She'd been drilled ever since she was a puppy, yet she too had gone back on her oath; she'd gone out of her mind.

Inside the barracks it was the hottest it had ever been that winter: by now they were no longer trying to make the coal last. The coal was melting and the stove belching greedily, shooting out sparks. The fire was crackling and roaring – it sounded as though the barracks was leaking, while above it torrential rain poured down, drumming on the roof. Exactly like when it buckets down with rain, it seemed that the square, the very ground itself, was on fire, and everything was either melting or roasting. Khabarov stood alone in the crimson glow of the stove, burnt by its light to the colour of earthenware. It was as if he wasn't there, although he had come in ages ago. On that day, time stood still, although it's true it was closer to evening, which had set in early as it does in winter, almost in the middle of the day. The entire company had gathered in the barracks. The bunks had been shifted closer to the blazing stove, but there was not enough room on them so people were stretched flat on the floor. The ones who had climbed down from the watchtowers were asleep, huddled up to their machine guns, keeping warm. It was peaceful and quiet, like in a hospital. In this hush, three soldiers were awake, sitting on a bench that was just about rammed into the stove; perhaps they had already managed to snatch some sleep. One of them glanced at the captain and shifted up; another just as unseeingly held out a cup of hot liquid to him, and the captain had to take it.

Set back down on the stove, the kettle began to crackle from the great heat: there was no more water in it. One of them hissed to another, 'Are you blind or something? Go bring some more snow, or it will burn.'

'I can see . . . ' the other replied, but he did not move. Then one of these mates stood up, seemingly an extra one, forgotten about. He grabbed the kettle angrily and vanished into the darkness.

'Lads, what are you up to? You have to do your duty, after all, or else it will all fall apart . . . ' said the captain, timidly. One of the more bad-tempered soldiers voiced his opinion: 'You can't do anything to us. Best help us, or we'll kick you out, as well. You know, we used to be daft but we've got cleverer. When we demand what's ours, we'll get it.' At this, from the shadows, from that dark pile into which the rows of bodies had amassed, there came a shout. 'So what are you waiting for, Khabarov? Do you want to stay alive, you son of a bitch? Well get the hell out of here, then, while you still can!'

The captain went back to his office; there was no other place for him. He sat at the icy desk, to which everything, right down to the paraffin lamp, had frozen solid. He lit the lamp, which sputtered and flickered. The captain looked at it, not knowing how much paraffin it had left. He was just waiting for the lamp to go out, thinking about it sluggishly, procrastinating, but the wick continued burning . . .

In the morning Khabarov was woken by the freezing darkness, and went to shovel snow in the square;

everyone in the barracks could hear his shovelling. Once he'd dealt with that, he started chipping out coal in the shed for the coming day, and they all heard the bangs of the crowbar ringing out. They knew, they heard, but they did not come outside. They chewed on dry, mouldy noodles, there being nobody to cook them.

The captain, white with snow, appeared bearing a scuttle full of coal. The stove had long since cooled to a deathly quiet. Khabarov got a little flame going and tenderly added coal. It started cooing, and caught light. When the warmth had set in, he stood by the blazing stove, which was thawing out the space around it, creating a widening circle of damp. He said to the men now warming themselves in the barracks, 'For the last time, believe my promise. I will go and fetch the wages. They will entrust me with the money, don't doubt that; as long as the company carries out its duty and does not mutiny. Give me two days, we'll get it sorted, and then it will be springtime. Come the spring, we'll have everything!' That day, they did not shovel the snow from the square, because the captain had done it. The day was more like dusk, and what's more, a blizzard set in, whirling and shaggy and twirling in solitude on the twilit steppe.

No one came to see Khabarov off, but he was glad to be left alone in the world. He set off in his felt boots and sheepskin coat, with a bottle of spirits stuck down the front, the one thing he had taken for himself. The bottle was just as much government property as the sheepskin; Khabarov had been given it by the medical officer in place of medicines and hospitals. That bottle comprised all his luggage, and it was surprisingly light, considering it provided him with drink, warmth, wellbeing and comfort: not so much a bottle as a mother. Taking a swig for the road, the captain walked and walked along the snowy ridge of the narrow-gauge rails, going ever deeper into the indistinct distance. Again and again he turned back towards the camp, to wave goodbye once more. Although he hadn't wanted to trouble the men to come and see him off, they spent a long time parting with him: even on that twilit day you could see a long way from the watchtowers. And so the captain did wave, thinking that the soldiers were looking out for him from the towers. The sentries could indeed make him out: there he was, crawling along crookedly, like an ant, and when the captain was lost from view, hidden by the snowstorm, they began to wait for him to come back.

The blizzard cheered Khabarov. Sheaves of snow formed flurries in the storm; they bustled and whirled, and from that white thread they instantly wove snow-white shawls with frilly edges, which flew in the wind, capering and dancing about. Here Khabarov took another swig from the bottle, not knowing when he would get there.

Having left the settlement, Khabarov was no more than halfway along the route to Stepnoi before he got lost on the steppe; by now, even in his mind, he was no longer aiming for Ugolpunkt but drowning in these blizzard-struck expanses. The captain had chosen the simplest route for his hike, which was also the airiest. He had been walking along the narrow-gauge track, or the ski-track it formed, which did indeed lead to Ugolpunkt. The direction was clear, like a diagram, but as it ran through the snow and blizzard, it began to spin in the air. Khabarov walked towards the station halt for so long that more than once he thought he had strayed from the tracks. Slinking away, the snowy track slipped out from under his feet and carried itself off ever further, and he was forever sliding off to the side, unable to keep up with it. Khabarov recognised the halt from the charred beams sticking out of the snowdrifts.

At some point then, at the Stepnoi junction, he suddenly panicked that he wouldn't make it to Ugolpunkt: the distance that had opened out before him was so great, not to mention the coming snowstorm. And here Khabarov took another swig from the bottle as he made it to the top of the snowy rampart that the railway embankment had become, but he didn't take a single step along it. The very moment he began thinking about the direction he should take to reach Ugolpunkt, everything in his head began whirling round like a wheel. Unsure which way to head, the captain looked in both directions as they twirled and danced, but he simply could not bring himself to choose one over the other, afraid, and becoming ever more so, of getting it wrong. Drowsily, he sat down on the spot, desperately trying to remember the right way to go. He came to just as the skies began to darken. The unfettered wind had whipped up a merry, drunken snowstorm, a proper blizzard. That wind seemed stronger than everything else, than either the snow or the harsh cold. It had shattered the winter! The air had built up great masses of snow, which were smashing themselves to pieces in the dark, carving themselves up into rumbling shards. And the captain recognised in those rumbles the blowing of the Buran; the Buran used to appear in the most placid steppe to collect little debts, but so many years had passed since it last came . . .

If the captain was to survive, he had either to wait or to crawl back to the settlement; but then, in the knowledge that should the people there not already know of the Buran, they would nevertheless soon be feeling its blasts themselves, he crawled out of his hole in the snow and forced his way a little further. He had no idea where he was going, but the thing was not to move backwards. He walked and crawled and dragged himself along, and paused to get his breath back, but when he no longer had the strength to keep moving forwards, he lay down and mourned that he could not, although he was not sorry for himself. Getting to his feet in a moment of lucidity, he could not work out what he was doing there. He stopped, but once more set his face into the scouring, icy firmament and forced himself on. At one point, he realised that his bottle of spirits had vanished in the Buran. At another, after a hazy period, he understood that he was missing his fur hat. But the captain did not intend to let himself freeze over, to die in that spot, and he pushed himself onwards because, or so it seemed, people had faith in him. Like a draught-horse, he dragged his frost-bitten legs. Like a river drags its icy waters, he dragged his frostbitten belly, and by now it seemed to him that he was hauling along the entire earth, the entire weight of the earth with its forests and seas. And then he crawled out of his sheepskin coat, was violently sick, and crawled on a bit more, still alive, still breathing . . .

Somewhere along the way, his life gave out. The captain himself no longer wanted to crawl onwards. In his last moments of lucidity, Khabarov delved under the crust of the snow; the top layer in that particular place turned out to be thin and fresh. He sank down into the loose snow so deeply that the roaring of the Buran faded away. There in the warmth, the sounds of the wind muffled by the snow, and warm at last, he dozed off. And then, painlessly and without waking, he died, and so never even knew for sure that he had.

The Buran raged over the steppe for three impenetrable days, then cleared in a matter of minutes. The steppe was covered by a calm, even, unbroken surface, and the light reflected by this surface, while sickly, was unbelievably clear; it poured out over the scarcely living expanse. Some of the sentry posts had not been abandoned at all; they had been taken up by men who had faith in the captain. The company had stood firm. It sometimes happened that stool pigeons and other such wicked personages would run across from the camp to the guardhouse, imagining that the *zeks* were about to do them in. The sentries let them through, and they sat in the corners, scared.

A great many things were destroyed by that Buran in Karabas; the soldiers could hardly recognise it when they emerged, but all were cheered by at least being able to see the sky, and nothing could contain their joy, for it was tired of being confined.

10

FOR GLORY, AND FOR
THE PEACE OF HIS SOUL

Not a word was said to the public about the natural disaster that struck regions of northern Kazakhstan, but leaving aside these regions, for a while it seemed that burials were everywhere, and the smoke from the funeral fires lay so thick you might easily have hung a hammer in it. Meanwhile, wherever it was applicable and for local use only, an expression became current: 'the Buran belt', by which was meant the lands that had been ravaged and destroyed by the extreme weather.

For a little while longer, Karabas was cut off from the outside world: telegraph poles had been toppled by the Buran over an extent of many kilometres and the company's radio transmitter was out of action. Helicopters appeared in the skies over the settlement and dropped supplies, which maintained life in the camp. The *zeks* rebuilt one of the barracks for themselves, where a small number of sentries kept them under guard. There was no work to be done; the camp was run by the warders. The soldiers elected a leader, one of their own, whom they respected. The most pleasant weather set in, and there was enough to eat in what was supplied. They didn't think about the captain, as sometimes happens when a man leaves but is due to come back, and everyone is so certain of this that they actually forget about him. A quiet, inspiring way of life took hold in the settlement, one that the men in it had never before experienced, which was surprising, if you recall that they had been born for such a life. Everything they needed dropped down from the sky without delay, and amid the devastation they lived more peacefully and ordinarily than ever, there being no forced labour or drilling. But then, from the direction of Stepnoi, there came an unexpected convoy. From Karabas, they saw that columns of men were moving towards them in good order, albeit floundering through snow up to their bellies, while behind them tractors were dragging logs, coils of barbed wire, barrels of diesel oil and warm shelters.

With the column of soldiers came officers, too, who were surprised to find that all this time there had been no commanding officer in the settlement. 'So where's your commander?'

'He went to fetch our pay.'

'Lucky him, living a life on what others have provided!' The officers were from an escort unit and could not hang about for long. The escort had been ordered to transport the prisoners to secure camps, while in Karabas itself they would leave a garrison of soldiers and craftsmen, who were supposed to restore all the damage by the spring.

They sorted out the *zeks*, signed for them, then led them along the narrow-gauge track in one great contingent, using tractors to clear the way right up to the halt, where they loaded the prisoners up onto the platforms. There they were set to work, passing down the supplies of wood, metal, boxes of nails and brackets, cement, bricks, lime and foodstuffs that were there awaiting onward transit. Strange people bustled round, shouting orders. But they all fitted in soon enough.

The work did not stop, even at night. There were enough people to form a legion: it was a wild, wide contingent, like a gypsy camp. Fires burned, guard dogs howled, sometimes there were gunshots. The little engine shuttled between Stepnoi and the camp: carrying a motley cargo one way, and returning packed with people. The bright, white night rocked, while this swarm of ants scurried all around. Arriving at the pick-up point, the engine poured out diesel fumes, like a ship. There were many volunteers: they had been selected from around the region and gradually brought into the settlement; they were labourers, real men.

You would not believe how friendly and cordial those days were, when Karabas was being stripped down and rebuilt; the jovial chatter was unending. The place teemed with people; everything came together. There was a tale you'd not pass on – you'd never credit it – of another incident from those days, concerning a man, the camp engine driver; you know, the old bloke with the gammy leg. He took pleasure from diesel fuel, and had acquired a source of this pleasure. He was no more than a camp louse, but he had a high opinion of himself, what with being an engine driver. The old man's heart used to sing as he saw out his term on the camp shunter, running on government-supplied diesel, telling perfect strangers, more often than not the labourers, 'I feel sorry for this machine. She'll die if she's not set to work. She needs looking after, just like a cow, and she needs the same kind of love.'

The old fellow had respect for the labourers, seeing as they weren't scared of hard work and they took an interest in the mechanics of his shunter, and because they did not begrudge a man – that is, him – a bit of tobacco. And this shunter driver took such a shine to these blokes who had come in from elsewhere that he would go off with them for a bite to eat or for a smoke break as though he was a labourer himself. So only at night did he part from them, heading back into his barracks at the camp, under lock and key, while the others spent the night at liberty in the army barracks, where they had rebuilt the roof and generally restored order as speedily as if it were their own home. And somehow, one day, the shunter driver did not go back for roll-call in the barracks, but went instead like a free man with the other blokes; he sat with them chatting over a drop of vodka, and lay down to sleep in the army barracks, where they gave up a bunk and mattress for him. And during this time they wouldn't have looked for him in the camp barracks anyway: the warders had got used to the fact that the engine driver worked at night as well. Old Pegleg had no kind of escort accompanying him, they just kept track of where he was by eye, like a little child; and anyway, what with the job he had, he was always in sight. That night, the old bloke did not close his eyes for excitement at spending the night among free men, who not only hadn't driven him out but had given him a mattress. He lay there, tossing and turning, nearly waking everyone up. 'What's troubling you?' one of them asked.

'Can't sleep, I could smoke a rollie, you know . . . '

'Smoke one, then. Here's a light, and some baccy.' Well then. He had a smoke, in the cold, out of respect for those asleep inside. Then he sat quietly over a drop to drink, and stayed like that till the very morning: he'd lie down, then have a smoke, then a drop to drink . . . If it had been a church, they'd have been reading matins when the engine driver walked back into the camp; everyone else was still asleep. The warder asked him, as he was letting him into the barracks, 'And just where did you manage to get pissed?' The engine driver replied, 'We're not drinkers, we've been working . . . ' And in the morning, back to work. The blokes called out to him, 'Where did you slope off to, in the night?'

'I'm supposed to be in the prison barracks.'

'Well, obviously! But don't let it upset you!'

During those days, they didn't start looking for Captain Khabarov. The settlement managed to set itself to rights, and emptied of people. They gave out the overdue wages, and that's when they remembered the captain – when there was no one to receive his pay!

So much time had passed. If the captain had kept walking tirelessly, he could have gone right round the world and so back to Karabas. Once they'd searched around a bit, but not found him present, a report went from the battalion to the regiment that the company commander had gone AWOL.

When this report reached the Special Department and came into the hands of Skripitsyn, he realised that there was no way the captain would have run off somewhere; if he was missing, that meant he was dead. He kept on at himself, under his breath, 'He would have died, regardless.' Stepping into action, Skripitsyn declared the captain AWOL, then began searching for his remains, being the only person who knew that Khabarov could not be among the living, since the life or death of some captain meant nothing to the regiment.

It was he who circulated written portraits of the vanished officer: 'Officer missing: medium height; strong build; thick dark hair, shot with grey; prominent forehead; wide oval face; moustache; prominent and fleshy nose and lips; eye colour unknown; no distinguishing features.' Then he made his way to Karabas, setting himself up in the administrative office and conducting constant interrogations, as though thirsting to find out everything about the captain that the man himself had concealed while still alive, and about what the soldiers being questioned were hiding: the truth about his death.

But there weren't many men left in Karabas who had lived through the Buran: some were in hospital, others had been replaced. The few survivors tried to tell the Special-Department agent that when the wages had not arrived on time, the captain had set out on foot for Ugolpunkt, while the Buran had blown in on the settlement that very night. The remaining soldiers admitted no guilt, even though Skripitsyn tried to squeeze the truth out of them, being party to allegations from the prison warders that there had been a mutiny in the company and the soldiers had refused to do their duties. And then Skripitsyn realised that it was Captain Khabarov himself who was covering for the people under him, and that he had come up with the idea of dying deliberately in order to save them from the courts, even at the price of his own life.

Despite coming away empty-handed, Skripitsyn did not call off the search for the body. Although the circumstances of Khabarov's death were now clear to the Special-Department agent, he searched for the missing captain's remains with even greater energy, as though he might be able somehow to get one step ahead in something important. Finding someone in the vast snowy steppe was akin to resurrecting them. And when Skripitsyn was informed that nothing had been found in the latest search area, he made himself scarce, as though he himself were the corpse. Whenever it was timidly suggested that they might never find the captain at all, that he might have been eaten by wolves or foxes, as happens to all the other carrion on the steppe, Skripitsyn would erupt, and the search, which had been winding down, would carry on once more at a dizzying pace.

Another thing that played on the agent's nerves was the fact that Khabarov's hat and sheepskin jacket had been found: the first on the steppe, over Kulunda way, and the second in the little town of Karakalinsk. Both were recognised as property of the regiment and items the captain had been wearing when he left the settlement. And if you believed for one moment that the captain had been in both those places, which were about a hundred kilometres distant from one another, then searching for him truly did seem pointless, for no one could track down a man like that.

Then came a weekday at the very end of March. There was still plenty of snow on the ground; it seemed as though winter had hidden in the snow and was secretly keeping it cold, which was why the drifts still seemed to tower like boulders. But by now, warm sunlight was playing over its firm surface. The air was so warm it felt stuffy. As though there was not enough of it for the drifts themselves, the snow became porous, breathing. Half the company was out on guard duty while, in the barracks square, the soldiers who were off duty for now were messing about, building snowmen and hurling snowballs at them. When the fun wore off, it came into their heads to let the guard dogs out, so that they, too, could mess around, running about heedlessly in the square. This made the soldiers happier again, as they flung snowballs at the dogs. When they started rounding them up, the thrill of the chase wore off. The dogs had gone wild in their aimless running about, and no longer heeded any commands. They set about rummaging in the snow, even swallowing it, and then they were forgotten, until a guard dog's howl suddenly rang out through the barracks and did not then subside: in a snowdrift right by the barracks wall, the guard dogs had dug up the body of Captain Khabarov. They were howling and whining; you'd have sworn they recognised him.

The captain was curled up into a ball, just as he had fallen asleep under the snow, and because he had slept soundly for such a long time, there was no power on earth that could unbend him and straighten him out. His sinews had turned into steel hawsers. They carried him like that into the barracks and set him down by the stove, curled into a ball. All around there was quiet, as though the men were trying not to disturb him. In all that time he had not changed, being preserved by the cold. Some idiot turned up, saying with surprise, 'Ah, Khabarov has arrived.' But he hadn't arrived, he had left. And nothing more is known, now, about those men who clustered round him; neither how they make their living these days, nor anything else. In the homely warmth, Khabarov began gradually to thaw. From beneath him ran a pure liquid, like tears. And then it seemed that he was a piss-artist, lying in a filthy puddle. He turned a blueish-grey in the heat, while his tunic became irremediably slimy. They decided not to wait any longer, then, and quickly sent a report to the regiment, which immediately demanded to have the located captain sent on, so he would only spend the one night in the barracks.

However, that same evening, they ordered in a joiner from the camp: 'Go and measure him up, mate, so that we can pack the captain come the morning.' The joiner scratched his head and sucked in his cheeks as he sidled round the captain.

'What you need here is something to break his bones with, or you could put him in a sack . . . '

'Oi! We'll tear your legs off and stick you in a sack in a minute, you son of a bitch!'

The joiner groaned, but in the morning the soldiers found him cheered again, rolling a barrel along. 'Here, use this. It used to have pickled cabbage in. I've steamed it out. Just smell that, it couldn't be nicer. I can't think of anything else, even if you threaten to cut me up. It's all right, this here barrel; it's a good 'un.'

Giving in, the soldiers crammed the captain into the barrel and the joiner caulked it up. Four soldiers who had been told to accompany the cargo and answer for it set about carrying the barrel as if it were a coffin, and the joiner watched them go, laughing quietly to himself. Then they spat, to ease their conscience, and began rolling the barrel along the calm, still snowy steppe.

The snow under the barrel crackled as though it was frying, and indeed the air smelt of Pancake Day: spring had arrived, after the winter. Taking their time, and struggling with their burden as they tried to get onto the passing train, the soldiers did finally deliver their captain to Ugolpunkt, where the morgue and the battalion HQ were awaiting him, ready to put the last full stop to his dossier. The soldiers never once baulked at their load. If anything, they were proud of the barrel, with which they had saved their captain and themselves from the sickened glances of other people. Nobody met them in the town, although they had been promised a vehicle and some orderlies. Once they had smoked their way through a packet of cigarettes – which was all they had between the four of them – the comrades decided to roll the barrel themselves to the battalion: it could make the men there sick now, for all they cared.

But along that same side street, without any idea what was in store for him, walked Ilya Peregud, released from the guardhouse. As it happened, he was walking towards the soldiers. He was strolling along, having long since forgotten about his expulsion by the captain. After he'd served a month for insubordination and drunkenness, he'd stayed in the guardhouse to see out another sentence; what's more, he'd done it in such a way that the prison governor nearly succumbed to alcoholism. Peregud was already fed up of walking along this street. Tormented, he looked out from under his grown-out topknot far into the back yards, on the off-chance he might get to put away a glass or two. He was hoping to spy a housewife who (you could tell by looking at her) ran her household the old-fashioned way, choosing only the best; or maybe the man of the house, no one out of the ordinary, who you could compliment on his woodshed, and on the logs themselves, at which he'd be bound to show a bit of generosity and pour a good man a glass; or, perhaps, he'd be sufficiently moved to set up all his bottles. Housewives in well-managed homes never mind pouring a drink for the sake of it; perhaps because they are women and women are like that. But somehow Ilya could not spot anyone: it was either children messing about in the snow, or those bloody old women shaking their dusty doormats into the air. By now he was thinking gloomily that he might as well go as far as the station itself to sniff its rusty ironwork and dream of drinking.

When he caught sight of the soldiers rolling the barrel, out of nowhere he had a vision of it full of beer. But it was impossible that soldiers would be rolling a barrel of beer along in broad daylight, and also Ilya had recognised, with some surprise, a few familiar faces. The comrades had recognised Peregud too, but they had stopped and were looking at him as if he were a ghost. Ilya could not contain himself. 'What's that barrel you've got, then?'

'It's sort of a coffin for Captain Khabarov. He's lying in it and we're rolling him to HQ. He's dead.' Skirting quickly round Ilya, they rolled the barrel on further. Peregud was rooted to the ground, and could only gaze helplessly after them while they hurried and hurried, gathering speed so that Ilya would not catch them up.

•

At peace with the world at last, the captain arrived at the regimental base with a fractured spine, his arms and legs twisted right off inside the coffin, and his stomach bristling with splinters, but they could not eradicate the smell of pickled cabbage. This remained just as strong in him as it had ever got, and when his casket was placed in the club for people to take their leave of him, both the honour guard and the line of people passing through luxuriated in a fragrant tickling of the nostrils, which made them want to sneeze.

No one could ever have imagined that one day a grave would be dug on the regimental parade square, but Captain Khabarov was buried there, on the base, with a hero's honours. The coffin was brought out onto the square, in full view of the serried ranks, who looked on, motionless. Behind the coffin came the regimental colours, dipped in salute, as though they were planning to bury these, too; they were just as red and solitary as the coffin. Skripitsyn uttered a speech at the edge of the still-empty grave, which acted as an echo chamber, making his voice carry over the entire square. They listened to the Special-Department agent listlessly, as though the personality in question aroused no interest in the servicemen, and at this the lopsided little man who looked more like a woman started speaking more fiercely, in paroxysms, and his final words were vented in a scream, 'Farewell, comrade Khabarov! You will remain in our hearts!'

The lid was placed on the casket, which was lowered into the grave, and the staff officers threw down handfuls of soil. Gun volleys burst out, spreading clouds of gunpowder smoke over the parade ground, which had been quite cheerless enough beforehand; these clouds meant that no one could see the grave being filled in with earth nor the tin rocket with a star at its tip that was planted in it. The regimental orchestra struck up a march and the regiment filed past, paying their last respects. They had already marched past in parade order when Skripitsyn interrupted the band with a peremptory shout and, in full view of Degtiar, who remained silent, he ordered the regiment to go back to the start and march past again, because they had not been trying, they had gone by poorly. This was a shock to those in the ranks, which had by now become rather mixed up. The officers grew angry and ran about, shoving the soldiers from behind: 'You sons of bitches, I want to feel the ground shake!' And the troops slammed down their boots like hammers: they marched properly. After the parade, indifferent to all around him, a swaying, muttering Skripitsyn walked around the captain's grave, which was now deserted, and then, suddenly growing sober, he looked around and marched away.

Due to the captain's death, Senior Lieutenant Sokolskii was sent in his stead to serve in Sixth Company. There was nothing really unusual in this and no one felt sorry for him. However, three days or so after he'd been taken off by lorry to Karabas, the regimental commander's office began to stink. The smell seemed to emanate by some mysterious means from the collected works of the Party greats – and there were such a lot of these – that stood in rows on the bookshelves. Everyone pretended that there was no stink. The office was aired frequently, but it would have been odd to leave the windows open. All the same, they made their minds up to check, pulling out the first volume of *Das Kapital* at random, and smelling it to see if, maybe, the paper had started to rot, but it was white as snow and, if anything, it smelt of cloth. Dangerous rumours began to circulate within the regiment, and then spread even further afield. When the stink died down and disappeared, the fears it had inspired nonetheless remained, as did the gloom. A heavy sense of expectation hung in the air. And one day, in the depths behind the collected works, a cleaner who was busy dusting with great seriousness discovered a slab-sided glass in which a turd had dried out into a rock; it had been put there by none other than Sokolskii: the only way he could enact his revenge.

Meanwhile, the earth on the captain's grave hadn't even time to settle before a terrible order hurtled through the army like a thunderbolt, taking everyone unawares and crushing them utterly: 'ALL UNITS ARE TO PLANT POTATOES AND FEED THEMSELVES.'

IVAN YAKOVLEVICH KHABAROV'S MISSIVE

Following Ivan Yakovlevich's death, none of his personal belongings or documents remained. Even the things that his corpse was clad in – the boots he was wearing, his equipment – were described and sequestered; an inventory was drawn up, as should happen when a man is struck from the lists or transferred from one unit to another. It is difficult to imagine that his threadbare tunic is still being worn by the next generation; clearly, the captain's tunic lay in the stores until it was written off, and then it was burnt, so that the mould would not spread. Not many people knew about a particular discovery, and those that had been aware completely forgot as the years passed. Yet a sheet of paper had been found on the captain when his body was searched; it had been folded into four, and the creases were worn. It was so thickly covered in writing it was as if it had been corroded by letters. This scrawl was appended to the case file that had hastily been opened on this corpse of dubious origin, when Khabarov had not yet been declared a hero. Very shortly after opening the investigation, it was closed, and all the strict rules were adhered to. Sealed and stamped, the file on Captain Khabarov was transferred with all its contents into the Karaganda military prosecutor's archive, classified as unimportant: to be kept for five years. At the end of this period, it was disposed of, along with many others of no use to anyone. Overwhelmed by this dusty paper torrent, the archivist for no apparent reason pulled out two forlorn documents that had been shut away in the file: one of them, citizen Khabarov's death certificate, went into the bin; but through a moment of carelessness, the other, which bore the legend that this was the 'written complaint of citizen Khabarov', acquired a life of its own. With meticulous attention to detail, the archivist discerned that the complaint had not been considered at all, and since the dead and the living had intermingled in his dulled mind, it seemed to him that someone had put this document on top of the file, rather than simply storing it inside the grey cardboard binding. So it went off on its travels, firstly around the prosecutor's office, then into further channels, but nowhere could it be dealt with satisfactorily, and so they grew rather afraid of it, quickly striking it from the record, until, in the midst of all the revelations being made around this time, it landed in a pair of sympathetic hands.

Sent to a newspaper that, at the time, was admired by the whole country for its bravery, it was printed as a reader's letter:

'When the regimental lorry is taken off its regular timetable, and then cancelled completely, a serviceman is left face to face with his troubles. He expends his energies on mere subsistence, rather than on his duties. He ekes out all his fats, and his supplies of bread and potatoes soon run out, or maybe they just brought him rotten potatoes to start with. But there's nowhere else to turn, so you just lay down and die. You read the papers: it's like everything here's done for people's benefit, they speak so respectfully to you. But take a look around, and it's worse than a prison camp. To occupy a state-owned flat, you have to have served ever so long. But when it's time to retire and you've lost all your health in the service, then you're no longer needed by anyone and they kick you out onto the bare steppe to die. They write that everyone is equal. But the commander, the boss, is still more important and can't be compared with the soldier at the sentry post. Almost the whole year long, daft orders hang over your head, and they strew broken glass under your feet, into your spirit and reason. There's no one you can tell: the civilian authorities have no reason to take you in. Yet you don't have the right to make a complaint to your own chain of command. And this regimental lorry, your sole link to the outside world. Who cancels it? That's the nub of the matter. The commanders, the bosses cancel it, who else? You sit in the barracks or the guardhouse, with no escape, and you think that the beasts in the forest have it better, it's all set up for a full life for them, there, while you're in some sort of prison camp, although you haven't robbed or murdered anyone. A few, select potatoes managed to grow, each as good as the next spud. It's not just that they took them away, it's that they went and let them rot pointlessly. All because I dared to do something without orders. They started trying to confuse me, saying you're a friend to such-and-such but an enemy to such-and-such. No one said thank you for the potatoes, everyone just swore at me for taking the land. They said I should follow orders. They said that was more important.'

The captain had written all of this down, pouring out his soul, and then he had forgotten all about his missive. He had carried it about with him, though, and delivered it to us himself, like a postman. If anyone had read the missive in the newspaper, they would have thought its author was still alive. What else could they have thought? But many people might not have read it. There were so many in those days, these complaints. We grew blind and deaf to them. For this reason, we inform the public, in addition to his next of kin, if any remain, that Ivan Yakovlevich Khabarov is dead. To his life, as described in this tale, and to his death, likewise, we append his missive. May his soul rest in peace.

LIST OF CHARACTERS

Balakaev
A stationmaster somewhere out on the steppe

Degtiar,
Petr Valerianovich
Adjutant, Karaganda regiment

Dobychin
General, inspecting various army units

Khabarov,
Ivan Yakovlevich
(Vania)
Captain of the Sixth Company

Kolodin, Aleksandr
(Sanka or Sasha)
Private in the Special Department

Korneichuk, Petr
Private in the Sixth Company

Peregud, Ilya
(Ilyusha)
Warrant Officer, Khabarov's second-in-command

Pobedov,
Fyodor Fyodorovich

Colonel, OC Karaganda regiment

Prikhodko

Private, a former interrogee of Skripitsyn

Sinebriukhov, Vilor

Commandant of the zone

Skripitsyn, Anatolii

Senior Warrant Officer, Special Department

Smershevich

Former head, Special Department

Sokolskii

Senior Lieutenant, Karaganda regiment HQ

Velichko, Vasil
(Vasia, Vasiliok)

Deputy Political Officer

GLOSSARY AND NOTE
ON MILITARY RANKS

araka   A spirit distilled from *kumis*, qv.

Batu Khan   The grandson of Chingis Khan, Batu
                  Khan led the Mongol conquest of Rus.
                  In Russian folk memory, this is remem-
                  bered as establishing the 'Mongol Yoke'
                  over the Russian people, which lasted
                  for some 250 years.

Buran   The great wind that blows occasionally
                  over the Kazakh steppe.

Kalmyk   One of the nationalities in the USSR.
                  Each officially recognised national-
                  ity had a corresponding 'homeland'
                  territory, in this case Kalmykia, on the
                  north-west shore of the Caspian Sea.

kumis   Fermented mare's milk.

Kyrgyz

Another of the nationalities in the USSR, their putative homeland was the Republic of Kyrgyzstan, in Central Asia. It was not unknown for ethnic Russians to look down on the other nationalities inhabiting the Soviet Union.

Special
Department

A section of the Soviet army dealing with counter-espionage and internal disciplinary matters. Its precursor, established during WWII, was SMERSH, an acronym formed from the Russian phrase 'Death to spies!' The literal meaning of Smershevich's name is 'son of SMERSH'.

verst

Traditional Russian measure of distance: equivalent to just over a kilometre.

zek

Camp inmate.

zone

That part of the camp complex where the *zeks* are actually confined.

Military ranks in the Soviet army do not map perfectly onto ranks in the British army: Captain, Colonel, General and so on are, however, functionally equivalent. So too is a unit's adjutant: Degtiar is here the senior officer responsible for the unit's administration.

The lower ranks are likewise straightforward: in both armies, the privates were at the lowest point in the hierarchy. Things become more complicated past the rank of sergeant: the British army recognises two classes of warrant officer (WO), but given the great variety of regimental traditions, there is a bewildering array of titles given to soldiers who are WO1 or WO2. Accordingly, in this story, I have settled on 'sergeant major' to denote the most senior of the non-commissioned officers among the conscripts (*starshina*, in Russian), while the 'warrant officers' are the non-conscripts of long service and – in theory – a particular military specialisation that demands longer than the standard two-year conscript term for preparation (*praporshchik*, in Russian). As Skripitsyn is at pains to point out, he is a senior warrant officer. Peregud is merely a warrant officer.

It should be noted that while these warrant officers were considered senior in rank to the sergeant majors, they were still 'other ranks', ie not commissioned officers. This helps explain Sokolskii's outrage at Skripitsyn's cavalier attitude to the regimental HQ.

Ian Appleby

Dear readers,

We rely on subscriptions from people like you to tell these other stories – the types of stories most UK publishers would consider too risky to take on.

Our subscribers don't just make the books physically happen. They also help us approach booksellers, because we can demonstrate that our books already have readers and fans. And they give us the security to publish in line with our values, which are collaborative, imaginative and 'shamelessly literary' (the *Guardian*).

All of our subscribers:

- receive a first edition copy of every new book we publish
- are thanked by name in the books
- are warmly invited to contribute to our plans and choice of future books

BECOME A SUBSCRIBER, OR GIVE A SUBSCRIPTION TO A FRIEND

Visit andotherstories.org/subscribe to become part of an alternative approach to publishing.

Subscriptions are:
£20 for two books per year
£35 for four books per year
£50 for six books per year

The subscription includes postage to Europe, the US and Canada. If you're based anywhere else, we'll charge for postage separately.

OTHER WAYS TO GET INVOLVED

If you'd like to know about upcoming events and reading groups (our foreign-language reading groups help us choose books to publish, for example) you can:

- join the mailing list at: andotherstories.org/join-us
- follow us on twitter: @andothertweets
- join us on Facebook: And Other Stories

This book was made possible thanks to the support of:

AS Byatt
Abigail Headon
Adam Biles
Adam Lenson
Adam Mars-Jones
Adrian May
Adrian Ford
Adriana Maldonado
Ailsa Holland
Ajay Sharma
Alan Bowden
Alasdair Hutchinson
Alasdair Thomson
Alastair Dickson
Alastair Gillespie
Alastair Kenny
Alastair Laing
Aldo Peternell
Alec Begley
Alex Gregory
Alex H Wolf
Alex Read
Alex Webber
    & Andy Weir
Alexander Bryan
Alexandra de
    Scitivaux
Alexandra de
    Verseg-Roesch
Ali Usman
Ali Smith
Alice Brett
Alison Macdonald
Alice Nightingale
Alice Toulmin

Alison Anderson
Alison Bennets
Alison Hughes
Alison Layland
Alison Scanlon
Alison Winston
Alistair Shaw
Allison Graham
Amanda Banham
Amanda Jones
Amanda Love Darragh
Amelia Ashton
Amy Crofts
Ana Amália Alves
    da Silva
Andrea Davis
Andrea Reinacher
Andrew Clarke
Andrew Marston
Andrew McCafferty
Andrew Robertson
Andy Chick
Angela Jane Fountas
Angela Jane
    Mackworth-Young
Angela Macfarlane
Angela Thirlwell
Angus MacDonald
Ann McAllister
Anna Britten
Anna Holmwood
Anna Milsom
Anna Vinegrad
Annabel Hagg
Anna-Karin Palm

Annalise Pippard
Anna-Maria Aurich
Anne Carus
Anne de Freyman
Anne & Ian Davenport
Anne Longmuir
Anne Marie Jackson
Anne Meadows
Anne Okotie
Anne Withers
Anne Woodman
Annette Morris
    & Jeff Dean
Annette Nugent
Annie Henriques
Annie Ward
Anoushka Athique
Anthony Messenger
Anthony Quinn
Aquila Ismail
Archie Davies
Asher Norris
Averill Buchanan

Barbara Latham
Barbara Mellor
Barbara Scott
Bartolomiej Tyszka
Ben Coles
Ben Smith
Ben Ticehurst
Ben Thornton
Bettina Debon
Brenda Scott
Brendan Franich

Brendan McIntyre
Briallen Hopper
Bruce Ackers
Bruce & Maggie
    Holmes
Bruce Millar

CT Rowse
Camilla Cassidy
Cara & Bali Haque
Cara Eden
Carl Emery
Carla Palmese
Caroline Barron
Caroline Gregory
Caroline Perry
Caroline Rigby
Caroline Thompson
Carolyne Loosen
Carrie LaGree
Catherine Nightingale
Catherine Whelton
Cecile Baudry
Charles Beckett
Charles Day
Charles Lambert
Charles Rowley
Charlotte Holtam
Charlotte Middleton
Charlotte Ryland
Charlotte Whittle
Charlotte Williams
Chenxin Jiang
Chris Day
Chris Gribble
Chris Lintott
Chris Stevenson

Chris Watson
Christina Baum
Christina Scholtz
Christine Luker
Christopher Allen
Christopher Butler
Christopher Marlow
Christopher Spray
Ciara Greene
Ciara Ní Riain
Claire Brooksby
Claire C Riley
Claire Tranah
Clara Crockatt
Clare Bowerman
    & Dan Becker
Clare Buckeridge
Clifford Posner
Clive Bellingham
Colin Burrow
Collette Eales

Daisy Aitchison
Damien Tuffnell
Dan Powell
Daniel Barley
Daniel Carpenter
Daniel O'Donovan
Daniel Gallimore
Daniel Hugill
Daniel James Fraser
Daniel JF Quinn
Daniel Ng
Daniela Steierberg
Dave Lander
David & Ann Dean
David Archer

David Attwooll
David Craig Hall
David Davenport
David Dougan
David Gould
David Hanson
David Hebblethwaite
David Hedges
David Herling
David Kelly
David
    Johnson-Davies
David Novell
David Roberts
David Wardrop
Debbie Pinfold
Deborah Smith
Denis Stillewagt
    & Anca Fronescu
Diana Brighouse
Dominic Charles
Duarte Nunes

E Jarnes
EJ Baker
Eamonn Furey
Echo Collins
Eddie Dick
Eileen Buttle
Elaine Martel
Elaine Rassaby
Eleanor Maier
Elizabeth Boyce
    & Simon Ellis
Elizabeth Cochrane
Elizabeth Draper
Elizabeth Polonsky

Elizabeth
& Tom Hanson
Ellie Michell
Els van der Vlist
& Elise Rietveld
Emily Evans
Emily Jeremiah
Emily Jones
Emily Rhodes
Emma Kenneally
Emma McLean-Riggs
Emma Teale
Eric Langley
Erin Barnes
Evgenia Loginova

Federay Holmes
Fiona & Andrew
Sutton
Fiona Quinn
Frances Chapman
Francesca Bray
Francesca
Calvocoressi
Francis Taylor
Francisco Vilhena
Freddy Hamilton

Gabriel Hummerstone
Gabriela Saldanha
Gabrielle Crockatt
Gabrielle Morris
Gale Pryor
Galia Loya
Garry Wilson
Gavin Collins
Gavin Madeley

Gawain Espley
Gay O'Mahoney
Geoff Thrower
Geoff Wood
George McCaig
George Sandison
& Daniela Laterza
George Savona
George Wilkinson
Georgia Panteli
Georgina Forwood
Gerald Peacocke
Gesine Treptow
Gillian Doherty
Gillian Jondorf
Gillian Spencer
Gillian Stern
Gloria Sully
Glynis Ellis
Gordon Cameron
Gordon Mackechnie
Grace Cantillon
Graham
& Elizabeth
Hardwick
Graham Lockie
Graham
& Steph Parslow
Guy Haslam

Hannah Falvey
Hannah
& Matt Perry
Hannah Perret
Hannes Heise
Harriet Mossop
Harriet Sayer

Helen Buck
Helen Manders
Helen McMurray
Helen Morales
Helen Riglia
Helen Simmons
Helen Wormald
Helena Taylor
Hélène Steculorum-
Decoopman
Helene Walters
Henrike Laehnemann
Henry Hitchings
Hercules Fisherman
Hilary McPhee
Howard Watson
Howdy Reisdorf
Hugh Buckingham

Ian Barnett
Ian Buchan
Ian Burgess
Ian McAlister
Ian McMillan
Ian Mulder
Ian & Wenna
Crockatt
Imogen Forster
Inna Carson
Irene Mansfield
Isabel Costello
Isabelle Kaufeler
Isfahan Henderson
Isobel Dixon

J Collins
J Ellis

JC Sutcliffe

Jack Brown

Jackie Andrade

Jacqueline Crooks

Jacqueline Lademann

Jacqueline Taylor

Jacqui Patience

James Barlow

James Clark

James Cubbon

James Mutch

James Portlock

James Upton

Jane Brandon

Jane Heslop

Jane Packman

Jane Tappuny

Jane Whiteley

Jane Woollard

Janet Dyson

Janet Mullarney

Jeffrey

    & Emily Alford

Jen Hamilton-Emery

Jennifer Higgins

Jennifer Hurstfield

Jenny Diski

Jenny Dover

Jenny Kosniowski

Jenny McPhee

Jenny Newton

Jerry Lynch

Jill Aizlewood

Jillian Jones

Jim Boucherat

Jo Elvery

Jo Harding

Joanne Hart

Jocelyn English

Joe Gill

Joel Love

Joel Norbury

Johannes Georg Zipp

John Conway

John Corrigan

John

    & Evanthe Blandy

John Gent

John Glahome

John Kelly

John Nicholson

John Oven

Jon Riches

Jon Lindsay Miles

Jonathan Evans

Jonathan

    & Julie Field

Jonathan Ruppin

Jonathan Watkiss

Jorge Lopez de

    Luzuriaga

Joseph Cooney

JP Sanders

Judit & Nigel

Judy Jones

Judy Kendall

Juju Sophie

Julia Humphreys

Julia Sanches

Julia Sandford-Cooke

Julian Duplain

Julian I Phillippi

Julian Lomas

Julie Begon

Julie Fisher

Julie Freeborn

Julie Gibson

Julie Van Pelt

Juliet Swann

Juliet Hillier

Juraj Janik

Justine Taylor

KL Ee

Kaitlin Olson

Karan Deep Singh

Karen Badat

Kasia Boddy

Katarina Trodden

Kate Griffin

Kate Leigh

Kate Pullinger

Kate Wild

Katharine Robbins

Katherine El-Salahi

Katherine Jacomb

Kathryn Lewis

Kathy Owles

Katia Leloutre

Katie Martin

Katie Smith

Katrina Ritters

Keith Alldritt

Keith Dunnett

Keith Underwood

Keith Walker

Kevin Acott

Kevin Brockmeier

Kevin Murphy

Kevin Pino

Kim Sanderson

Kristin Djuve
Kristina Fitzsimmons
Krystalli Glyniadakis

Lander Hawes
Laraine Poole
Larry Colbeck
Laura Jenkins
Laura Murdoch
Laura Solon
Laura Woods
Lauren Kassell
Lauren Roberts-Sklar
Lea Beresford
Leanne Bass
Leeanne O'Neill
Leni Shilton
Lesley Lawn
Linda Broadbent
Linda Foster
Linda Harte
Lindsay Brammer
Lindsey Ford
Lisa Pook
Liz Clifford
Liz
    & David Till
Liz Ketch
Liz Tunnicliffe
Lizzi Wagner
Loretta Brown
Loretta Platts
Lorna Bleach
Lorna Scott Fox
Lorraine Curr
Louisa Hare
Louise Bongiovanni

Louise Rogers
Lucinda Smith
Lucy North
Lyn Abbotts
Lynda Graham
Lyndsay Cockwell
Lynn Martin

M Manfre
Maggie Peel
Maisie
    & Nick Carter
Mandy Boles
Mansur Quraishi
Marella Oppenheim
Margaret Duesenberry
Margaret Jull Costa
Maria Elisa Moorwood
Maria Potter
Marie Schallamach
Marie Therese Cooney
Marieke Vollering
Marina Castledine
Marion Cole
Marion Tricoire
Mark Blacklock
Mark Howdle
Mark Richards
Mark Stevenson
Mark Waters
Martha Nicholson
Martin Brampton
Martin Hollywood
Martin Conneely
Martin Whelton
Mary Ann Horgan
Mary Bryan

Mary Haig
Mary Morris
Mary Nash
Mary Tara Marshall
Mathias Enard
Matt Riggott
Matthew Bates
Matthew Francis
Matthew Lawrence
Maureen Cooper
Maureen Freely
Maxime Dargaud-Fons
Michael Bagnall
Michael
    & Christine
    Thompson
Michael Harrison
Michael James
    Eastwood
Michael Kitto
Michael Thompson
Michelle Bailat-Jones
Michelle Purnell
Michelle Roberts
Miles Visman
Milo Waterfield
Minna Daum
Monika Olsen
Morgan Lyons
Moshi Moshi Records
Murali Menon

N Jabinh
Nadine El-Hadi
Nan Haberman
Nancy Scott
Naomi Frisby

Nasser Hashmi
Natalie Rope
Natalie Smith
Natalie Wardle
Nia Emlyn-Jones
Nicholas Holmes
Nick Chapman
Nick Nelson
   & Rachel Eley
Nick Sidwell
Nicola Cowan
Nicola Hart
Nicola Ruffles
Nina Power
Nuala Grant
Nuala Watt

Odhran Kelly
Oladele Olajide
Olga Zilberbourg
Olivia Heal
Omid Bagherli
Owen Booth

PD Evans
PM Goodman
Paddy Maynes
Pamela Ritchie
Pat Henwood
Patricia Appleyard
Patricia Francis
Patricia Melo
Patrick Coyne
Paul Cahalan
Paul Dettman
Paul Gamble
Paul Hannon

Paul Jones
Paul Myatt
Paula Ruocco
Paulo Santos Pinto
Peny Melmoth
Pete Ayrton
Peter Law
Peter Lawton
Peter Murray
Peter Rowland
Peter Straus
Peter Vos
Philip Warren
Phyllis Reeve
Piet Van Bockstal
Poppy Toland
   & Rob Palk
Pria Doogan

Quentin Webb

Rachel Henderson
Rachel Parkin
Rachel Pritchard
Rachel Sandwell
Rachel Van Riel
Rachel Watkins
Rebecca Atkinson
Rebecca K Morrison
Rebecca Moss
Regina Liebl
Réjane Collard
Rhian Jones
Richard Carter
   & Rachel Guilbert
Richard Dew
Richard Jackson

Richard Jacomb
Richard Martin
Richard Smith
Rishi Dastidar
Rob Fletcher
Robert
   & Clare Pearsall
Robert Delahunty
Robert Gillett
Robert Postlethwaite
Robin Patterson
Robin Woodburn
Ronnie Troughton
Rose Alison Cowan
Rose Cole
Rosemary Rodwell
Rosie Hedger
Ross Macpherson
Ross Walker
Ruth Ahmedzai
Ruth Clarke
Ruth Fainlight
Ruth Mullineux
Ruth Stokes

Sabine Griffiths
Sally Baker
Sam Byers
Sam Ruddock
Samantha Sawers
Samantha Schnee
Sandie Guine
Sandra de Monte
Sandra Hall
Sara D'Arcy
Sarah Bourne
Sarah Butler

Sarah Magill
Sarah Nicholls
Sarah Salway
Sarojini Arinayagam
Saskia Restorick
Scott Morris
Sean Malone
Sean McGivern
Seini O'Connor
Selin Kocagoz
Shan Osborne
Sharon Evans
Shaun Whiteside
Sheridan Marshall
Sigrun Hodne
Simon Armstrong
Simon Blake
Simon M Robertson
Simon Okotie
Simon Pare
Simon Petherick
Simon Wheeler
Sinead Fitzgerald
SLP
Sonia McLintock
Stefanie Freudenthal
Steph Morris
Stephanie Ellyne
Stephen Abbott
Stephen Bass
Stephen Pearsall
Stephen Walker
Steve Buzzard
Stewart MacDonald
Stewart McAbney
Stuart Condie
Sue Halpern

Sue Ritson
Susan Murray
Susan Tomaselli
Susana Medina
Susanna Jones
Susie Nicklin
Suzanne Fortey
Suzanne Kirkham
Suzanne Smith
Sylvie Zannier-Betts

Tamsin Ballard
Tania Hershman
The Mighty Douche
    Softball Team
Thomas Fritz
Thomas Reedy
Tien Do
Tim Russ
Tim Theroux
Tim Warren
Tina Andrews
Tina Rotherham-
    Winqvist
Tom Bowden
Tom Heel
Tom Long
Tom Mandall
Tom Russell
Tony Crofts
Tony & Joy Molyneaux
Torna Russel-Hills
Tracey Martin
Tracy Northup
Trevor Wald
Trish Hollywood

Vanessa Garden
Vanessa Nolan
Vanessa Wells
Victoria Adams
Victoria O'Neill
Vinita Joseph

Walter Prando
Wendy Knee
Wiebke Schwartz
Will Buck
    & Jo Luloff
William Black
William Evans
William G Dennehy
William Prior

Yvonne Overell

Zoe Brasier
Zoë Laughton

Current & Upcoming Books by And Other Stories

Title: *Captain of the Steppe*

Author: Oleg Pavlov

Editor: Sophie Lewis

Proofreaders: Sally Evans-Darby, Alex Billington

Typesetter: Tetragon

Set in: 10.5/15.25pt Swift Neue Pro, Verlag

Series and Cover Design: Joseph Harries

Format: B Format with French flaps

Paper: Munken Premium Cream 80gsm FSC

Printer: T J International Ltd, Padstow, Cornwall